TEMPTING MONTANA

PARKER KINCADE

Editor: Lacey Thacker

Cover Artist: Patricia Schmitt, Pickymeartist.com

NOTE FROM THE AUTHOR

Dear Reader,

Tempting Montana was originally published in Amazon's Kindle Worlds program as part of Elle James' Brotherhood Protectors world.

I have removed all elements linking this story to Elle's world, but no other story changes were made.

THANK YOU for reading the Martin Family and this Deadly Seven crossover series. I hope you enjoy the guys as much as I do.

~Parker

For Dodie, who inspired this story with a chainsaw. I love you, girl.

And for Booker. You're welcome.

PROLOGUE

Hoping her smile sounded more genuine than it was, Judith Abernathy answered her ringing desk phone with a pleasant, "Owen Jennings' office."

"Judith. It's Owen."

No shit, Sherlock. And because Owen wasn't in the office where he could see, Judith took great delight in performing a monumental eye roll. After eight years as the executive assistant to the senior partner of Jennings, Bradford & Mosley law firm, Judith could recognize Owen's number when it popped up on caller ID with nothing more than a glance. God forbid she break protocol by answering with a cheerful, personalized greeting when she knew it was him calling. She'd tried that once. There was a slip of paper in her employment file that ensured if she wanted to keep eating, she wouldn't try that nonsense again.

"Good afternoon, Mr. Jennings." Another ridiculous job requirement. It was okay for him to refer to himself as Owen when speaking to her, but she must address him formally. Because his money, power and position demanded more respect than her hard work and sweat.

"The courier," he said without preamble. "The flash drive...," the cell connection wavered, "left...desk. Have ... deliver ... Elizabeth King."

Judith read between the lines. Owen—Mr. Jennings—wanted her to get the flash drive from his desk and send it to Elizabeth King via courier. She'd done the task a hundred times before, but usually Mr. Jennings handed her the flash drive personally. He didn't like anyone in his office when he wasn't there, including his personal assistant.

Mr. Jennings just granted her a limited key to the kingdom, making Judith wonder if he had a glass or two of wine at lunch.

"I'll take care of it, sir. Anything else?" Oops. She hadn't meant to sound so terse.

"Yes, Judith. Several things," he replied in staccato, letting her know he noticed. "I need a moment to park."

"Of course." After all, she didn't have anything better to do.

Judith glanced at the stack of work she had to finish before she left for the day. She'd be lucky to make it home before dinnertime.

Mr. Jennings' voice boomed through the line again. "Make inquiries into upgrading Elizabeth's internet service to a speed sufficient enough to receive and send files in an timely manner."

She won't like that any more than she likes being called Elizabeth, Judith thought as she jotted down the task on her notepad. At least the cell connection had strengthened so she wouldn't have to ask him to repeat himself.

"Of course." Her standard reply. "I will email the information to you."

"On second thought, don't bother. I don't have time to deal with installers. Just take care of it. Find the fastest, most

reliable service and see that the upgrade is done immediately."

Treading carefully, Judith said, "Whichever service I
select will need Ellie's authorization to upgrade the service
at her house. Is that going to be a problem?"

Judith suspected it would be, but as always, she kept her
opinion to herself.

"Since the firm is paying for the service, *Elizabeth* will
give the authorization."

"All right. I'll take care of it."

"See that you do. Also, I'll be taking her to dinner
tomorrow evening. Call Truluck's and tell them to reserve
my usual table. Seven o'clock."

*She won't like that, either. Nor will the people who will get
their reservation at the premier seafood and steakhouse
bumped.*

"Yes, sir." And by sir, she meant asshole.

"I'm due in court." He hung up.

"You're welcome," she snarked into the dead line.
"Happy to be of service."

Judith sighed. Food. Mortgage. Electricity. The firm paid
her well, which was the primary reason she tolerated
Owen's holier-than-thou attitude.

Dreading the next task, Judith punched the button for
an open line and called the restaurant. By the time she
finished commiserating with the hostess over thoughtless
males, Mr. Jennings had his reservation.

She couldn't help feeling a bit sorry for Ellie, the name
Elizabeth preferred to be called. Ellie had been Mr.—to hell
with it—Owen's assistant before Judith. Eight years ago,
Ellie's mother developed a debilitating, terminal disease.
Refusing to allow strangers to care for her mom, Ellie struck
a deal with the partners to take on all the transcription work

for the office—making her a hero among the assistants—provided she could do it remotely.

The woman was a saint in Judith's book. For eight years, she selflessly cared for her mother, who passed away only six months ago, while working furiously to keep up with the demand from the office.

Owen took an unsettling interest in helping Ellie through the legalities of her mom's death—interest that now seemed to overflow into other, more personal areas. Internet service and dinner, indeed.

She would bet next month's salary Ellie hadn't agreed to either.

Judith pushed back her chair, circled around, and stood. She smoothed her skirt as she walked across the space that separated her desk from Owen's corner office. A flutter of unease tickled her belly as her hand landed on the doorknob. She had permission, damn it. She'd been in his office more times than she could count. Still, she glanced left, then right, before entering her boss's domain, as though she was about to commit a felony.

She stepped inside, leaving the door open. Owen's office was impeccably clean, not a paperclip out of place. Neat, organized stacks of files decorated the corner of the desk by the phone. A flash drive sat on top of the stack nearest the edge. Bingo.

Three steps in, her spiked heel caught on the carpet. Judith stumbled, the missed step causing her ankle to roll from its tall perch. With a cry of pain, Judith lost her balance. Her hip hit the corner of the desk. She tried to grab on to the edge to keep from falling, but her hand landed on the files instead. They scattered and fell to the floor along with the phone, while Judith managed to just barely escape the same fate.

Breathing heavily, standing on one foot with her back-side resting against the edge of the desk, Judith surveyed the mess.

"Oh, for the love of Pete."

She kicked off her shoes, hiked up her skirt, and eased her knees to the carpet. There was a piece of plastic on the floor. It looked like something that would be used to cover batteries in an electronic device. Glancing around the chaos on the floor, she saw the desk phone and picked it up. She placed the handset on the cradle—thankful it hadn't broken —and turned the phone over. Sure enough, the plastic piece fit over a small, empty compartment on the back. Her phone had the same feature—a place to store the extra length of a too-long phone cord.

She replaced the compartment cover and checked to make sure the phone still worked before placing it back on the desk.

The flash drive was on the carpet with the files, so she picked it up and placed that on the desk as well. Judith scooped the files into a pile. As she went to straighten them, another flash drive dropped from the stack.

She froze.

Well, crap.

She picked up the flash drive and compared it with the other drive she'd found. They looked exactly the same as every other drive she had sent to Ellie. Owen had said drive, right? Not drives, plural? The connection had been choppy, so he could've...

There was only one way to find out.

She quickly straightened the files and put them back on the desk, praying Owen hadn't put them in any particular order. She'd rather not have to explain her clumsiness.

Judith stood, grabbed her shoes, and hobbled back to

her desk. She inserted the first flash drive and called up the information. Audio files. Perfect. That's what she was looking for. She ejected the drive and inserted the second drive. Audio files. Hmm.

She clicked one of the files and Owen's voice sounded through her speakers. She listened just long enough to recognize the name of a corporate client and knew the audio was meant for transcription. She checked her watch. If she didn't get the courier there soon, the information wouldn't get to Ellie until late tomorrow instead of first thing in the morning. She thought about having to tell Owen she hadn't asked for clarification and therefore his instructions hadn't been carried out. That would not go well for her.

She didn't need to check every file. If one was meant for transcription, it was safe to assume they all were. She switched the drives and opened the first file. Owen's droning, dictation voice again. She stopped the recording.

Owen had said drives, plural. She had misunderstood because of the poor connection, right?

Time's-a-wastin'.

Making an executive decision, Judith shoved both drives into an envelope and called for a courier.

1

"You should have someone look at that cut above your eye. It looks nasty, Spaniard."

Booker Maldano flipped his buddy Roman the bird and shifted his ass on the hard, plastic seat underneath him. He motioned to the room at large. "We all look like we've been chewed up and spit out. I'll get checked out once we get some news."

The waiting room at Seton Medical Center had been packed, and it became even more so when Booker and his friends arrived. The cute chick behind the front desk had taken one look and promptly ushered them into a private waiting area so as not to scare the ailing folks of Austin.

With an average height of over six feet, Booker and his friends were an intimidating group on the best of days ... and today had been far from the best.

Booker fingered his injured eyebrow. A butterfly bandage or two—okay, three—and he'd be good to go. He glanced at the others. His team. His brothers. He wasn't the only one sporting damage. Roman Powers' knuckles were busted to shit. Sitting next to Roman, Sully Walsh nursed a split lower lip. Adam Casey leaned his back against the wall, pants stained with blood and appearing to favor his left side.

Across the room, Brandon Martin had his cell phone pressed against his ear, lips pressed into a tight line. That couldn't be good. Neither were Brandon's torn shirt and the blood that had dried in rivulets on his arm.

Noah Summers was the only one of them not visibly bleeding, but the way he repeatedly tipped a flask to his mouth and one-arm-hugged his midsection, Booker suspected Noah sported a broken rib or two.

Ketcher Novak, who was notably absent, rounded out their group. Their missing man had taken the brunt of the damage, having tangled directly with the guy who had taken Ketcher's woman.

Please let her be okay.

Ketcher had recently killed a Cuban drug lord down in Florida. Wounded during the operation, Ketcher had been ordered to lay low until he recovered. The younger brother of said drug lord promised retribution. Unable to locate Ketcher's whereabouts, the asshole had kidnapped Dr. Regan Daniels in an attempt to draw Ketcher out into the open.

Mistake number one.

The tactic had worked, but in his infinite stupidity the kidnapper hadn't counted on Ketcher coming with backup.

Mistake number two.

A few hours ago, they'd gone in and rescued Regan. Booker and the guys had provided cover and secured Regan while Ketcher showed that motherfucker what happened when you messed with one of their own.

Game over.

There was a reason Regan had dubbed them the deadly seven all those years ago in Afghanistan. Individually, they were good. Together, they were downright lethal. And they got the job done.

Days like today made Booker glad they were all out of the military. If they had been deployed and anything had happened to Regan ... Ketcher would've been ruined.

Booker ground his teeth, an ancient pain resurrecting in his chest. He knew about the helplessness of being thousands of miles away when life turned sideways. The frustration. The pain.

Oh yeah. He knew a little something about that.

Booker dropped his head back against the wall and closed his eyes. Life could change in an instant. Or rather, *lives* could change. Where one life changed, so goes another. And another. Booker had seen enough carnage to know the truth. Hell, right now *they* were an exercise in the ripple effect. Every man in this room would walk away changed forever if they didn't receive favorable news about Regan's condition.

But change wasn't always instantaneous, was it? Sometimes it was gradual. Sometimes it snuck up on a man like a thief in the night, stealing everything worth—

Someone dropped into the chair to Booker's left and nudged him.

"We might have a situation."

Brandon.

Booker rolled his head toward his buddy and cracked his lids. Booker had known Brandon for most of his life. They had gone to school together. Played varsity football together. Joined the military and served their country together. The history between them made it easy for Booker to read the guy. Brandon was hesitant. Concerned, but not wired for all-out detonation. Whatever the situation was, it wasn't likely to blow up in his face.

"What's up?"

God, he sounded as tired as he felt. And his eye was beginning to throb. He didn't need another problem right now. He needed to hear Regan was going to be okay so he could get the hell back to Montana and the life waiting for him there. If work and renovating a house he'd never occupy could be considered a life.

"Can you take a few extra days off?"

Annnd, so much for getting home.

Booker fought the urge to sigh as he dipped his chin. "James, my boss, is a good guy. He served. He understands brotherhood." And he wouldn't flinch if Booker had to stick around to help a buddy out.

James Kent owned Kent Protection Service. KPS had been Booker's saving grace. Separation from active duty was a challenging process. Acclimating to the rhythm of civilian life was hard enough. Try finding a job when your only work experience was drenched in sand and blood.

Booker had a family to consider. He'd almost given up hope of finding a job when James reached out to him. James was a retired Marine. His new mission was to give former military men and women a place to do what they did best—protect others. A phone call and a trip to Montana later, Booker had a new future.

"Work is slow right now," Booker said. "James was cool about giving me time to take care of things here. He won't balk if I'm a few days late getting back." Although Booker might, if Brandon didn't get on with the why of it.

"And your family? Will the delay affect the renovation?"

Irritation growing, Booker stared hard at his friend. He got the feeling he was being vetted for something, and it was starting to piss him off.

"Really, 'mano? That's how we're going to play this?"

The dickwad knew Booker wouldn't refuse whatever fucked up situation he had going on, regardless of how it would affect the construction timeline.

"Indulge me."

Booker blew out a breath. After he accepted the job with the Kent Protection Service, he used most of his savings to buy a forty-six acre hobby farm on the outskirts of Big Timber, a picturesque little town nestled between the Crazy Mountains and the Absaroka-Beartooth Mountains. The property boasted a four-bedroom house, a one-bedroom guest cabin, a three-stall barn, and a creek that ran along the western border.

Booker stayed in the cabin, where he would continue to live even after he moved his grandmother, mother, sister, and adolescent niece into the main house. Unfortunately, the house had been neglected for years and needed a total overhaul. Construction was well under way, but it would be months before the house was ready for inhabitants. In the meantime, the ladies would continue living together in Booker's childhood home on the outskirts of Austin.

"My family is fine. They, and the status of the renovation, are not for you to worry about. Both are my responsibility. I'm the one who'll decide how I spend my time, not you. Now, are we gonna keep dancing or are you going to tell me what's going on?"

Brandon's gaze darted around the room, looking everywhere but at him. "I'm not sure yet. I just got a call from a..." Brandon hesitated, making Booker's spidy sense go on high alert. "A friend." Brandon leaned forward, resting his forearms against his thighs. He glanced back at Booker. "Look, it might be nothing. Until I know for sure, I'd like you to stick around."

"Is it Nat?"

Natalie Cordova was an honorary member of their group and the only one of them still active military, although no one knew who she actually worked for or what she actually did. She and Brandon were ... close. Friends and fuck buddies for years, but as far as Booker knew, that's as far as it went.

Brandon shook his head. "No. As far as I know, she's fi —" The ding signaling a text drew Brandon's attention. As Brandon glanced at the screen, the new sense of urgency surrounding the guy had all eyes turning their way.

"Fuck. We gotta go."

"Startin' to get pissed off at all the mystery, 'mano."

The door to the waiting room flew open and Ketcher waltzed through.

"Three minutes," Brandon muttered and surged to his feet.

Booker followed suit, gaze on Ketcher as a cheesy-ass grin split the man's bruised mug.

"Regan's fine. Better than fine. She's perfect. A few bumps and bruises, but nothing..." Ketcher's voice cracked. "Nothing permanent."

Cheers and oorah's filled the room, followed by back slaps and a round of man hugs.

Booker's knees wobbled in relief. He knew the pain of losing someone he loved. He crossed himself, touched his first two fingers to his lips, and then pointed them toward the heavens with a silent prayer of gratitude that his friend would be spared the same heartache.

While he was at it he offered up another prayer, hoping the Big Guy wouldn't fault him for hedging his bets.

After all, he only had one minute left and had no idea what waited for him when the time ran out.

BOOKER FOLLOWED Brandon away from the joyous atmosphere of the waiting room, an undeniable sense of foreboding increasing with every step. Clearly the lack of sleep was making him punchy, so he shoved the worry aside. Whatever his friend needed, Booker had his back. No question.

When they reached the epicenter of the ER, Brandon slowed. "Room 8?" he asked as they approached a nurse's station.

A nurse pointed them in the right direction, and in less than a minute they stood outside a floor-to-ceiling sliding door made of glass and chrome.

Brandon glanced at the number over the doorway. "This is it."

The guy sounded almost ... apologetic. And since Booker didn't know what "it" was, he said, "Do you want me to stay out here until you determine whether you'll need me to hang around or not?"

"You'll want to hang around." He clapped a hand on Booker's shoulder, squeezing once before letting go.

Seriously, what the hell? The guy was weirding him out.

Brandon went through the door first. Booker hung back in the doorway, prepared to guard against any unwanted interruptions while his buddy assessed the situation.

Bright fluorescents illuminated the room. Machines and wires ran from every inch of the wall behind the hospital bed. Rolling carts filled with medical supplies occupied the left side of the room. A sink and cabinets on the right.

A nurse appeared to be cleaning a wound on the crown of a woman's head. Although the nurse's arm obscured the woman's profile, Booker knew she was a woman from the delicate curve of her back and the brief glimpse he got of a small, round breast as the nurse shifted position.

Brandon kneeled in front of her. They spoke in tones too low for him to understand, but there was something distinctly familiar about the girl. The subtle tilt to her head as Brandon spoke. The quiet lilt of her response.

"All finished," the nurse said and straightened. "The doctor will be in after he reviews the X-rays they took when you got here." When she stepped away from the patient Booker's heart stopped pumping.

The first thing he thought was maybe he'd gotten hit harder than he realized, because no way was he seeing what he thought he was seeing. His mind must be playing tricks on him. The woman sitting on the edge of the bed ... it couldn't be.

He blinked hard. Refocused.

And for the second time in his life, the world tilted on its axis.

"Ellie." The name caught in his throat, its syllables rusted from lack of use.

She turned and *fuck*, her beauty sucker-punched him. Booker drank in her image like a man starved. And wasn't he? For twelve years he'd been denied those dark chocolate eyes. Her delicate nose and perfect lips.

Her eyes widened and she bolted to her feet. "Brandon, what...?" Her expression morphed from surprised to decidedly panicked. "W-why is he here?"

"Is there a problem?" the nurse asked, her gaze darting between the occupants of the room.

"We're fine." Tacking on a smile that no doubt melted panties, Brandon said, "Could you give us a minute?"

The nurse's stance softened. She looked to her patient for confirmation. At Ellie's stilted nod, the nurse slipped out of the room, but not before shooting Brandon an inviting smile.

Whatever. The guy could score on his own time. Booker slid the door shut, using those precious seconds to get his head straight. It wasn't enough. Wasn't near enough. He turned and stepped deeper into the room.

"What the holy hell is going on here?"

Ellie backed up a step; her hand flying to her throat as though she expected Booker to strangle her.

And he might. He *just fucking might*.

Her gaze darted between the two of them, finally settling on Brandon. "That's what I'd like to know. Why is he here?" Her volume and shoulders grew in strength. "And why do you both look like you've been in some kind of accident?"

"He's here because I asked him to come. We can't get into the rest of…"

Booker tuned out, not giving two shits what kind of explanation Brandon had to offer. Right now, he was more interested in the girl.

Head-to-toe and back, he studied her, still not convinced his brain wasn't playing tricks on him. She looked different. Thin. Too thin. Hair was shorter. Short enough to leave the delicate line of her neck exposed. What was that color? Mahogany? There was probably some fancy name for the shade that looked red one minute, purple the next, depending on the light. A plain white tank hugged breasts that were smaller than he remembered, but no less perfect. Faded denim rode low on her hips and covered the legs he could still feel wrapped around his waist.

Son of a bitch.

Booker's lungs went on lockdown as heat rose in his chest. Years' worth of the emotional sludge he'd worked hard to repress oozed to the surface and brought his temper along for the ride.

He'd had a shitty fucking day. Sure, they'd saved Regan and she was going to be okay—big win—but in the process he'd gotten his head bashed with the stock end of a rifle, earning himself one hell of a headache. He was running on virtually no sleep. He couldn't remember the last time he ate. Now, his best friend had deliberately deceived him. And was that a bruise forming on the side of Ellie's face?

Christ.

It was Booker's final straw. He marched forward, clamped a hand around Brandon's arm and spun the guy to face him. Booker knew what he was about to do was a terrible idea, but in that moment no force on earth could've stopped him. Consequences be damned, Booker hauled off and punched his friend on the jaw.

Brandon stumbled sideways, catching himself on the edge of the counter with a curse.

Ellie—*his* Ellie—cried out with alarm and stepped between them. "Stop! What do you think you're doing?"

Brandon straightened and moved his jaw back and forth, apparently checking for damage. Eyes blazing, Brandon jabbed a finger in his direction. "Considering the circumstances, I'm gonna let you have that one."

Let him, his ass. If he wanted to dish out another hit, he'd damn well serve it up. And Brandon would take it because god*damn.*

Booker wanted answers and he wanted them now.

"Motherfucker," Booker ground out. "You didn't think it was need-to-know that your *situation* was my fucking wife?"

Fuck answers.

Booker hit him again.

2

This was the worst day of Elizabeth King's life. Considering the perpetual shit storm of her existence, that was saying something.

She'd overslept and in her rush, left the house without her wallet. In her sprint from the front door to the car, the courier who delivered her weekly envelope from work had delayed her even more. On the way to an important job interview her car had overheated, the engine puffing smoke like an old-school locomotive. When she called from the side of the road to reschedule the interview, she'd been informed the job she desperately wanted had been filled and *didn't she get the voicemail about the cancellation?*

No. No, she hadn't.

It had taken her thirty minutes to walk to the nearest gas station—barefoot, because she was not making the trek in heels—where she purchased a gallon of water with change she'd found in the console of the car. Another hour to walk back, fill the radiator, and proceed with her long list of overdue errands. By the time she'd arrived home, the better part of the afternoon had disappeared.

As if she hadn't dealt with enough, she discovered—too late—there was a burglar inside her house. Thank goodness he hadn't done worse, but the man had roughed her up enough to warrant the trip to the ER ... where she now stood with the ex-husband she hadn't seen or heard from in twelve years and who looked one pinkie twitch away from going in for round three with Brandon.

Yep. Worst. Day. Ever.

Brandon recovered quickly from the second punch, but his vile curse still echoed in her ears. The tension in the air made Ellie wish she could disappear. Or at least go back to before she called Brandon so she could make a different choice in her bid to not be alone. Maybe call Brandon's younger brother Alec, instead. She wasn't close with him, but Alec was cool. He definitely wouldn't have shown up carting two-hundred-plus pounds of her emotional baggage along with him.

Brandon spit into the trashcan, and then wiped the back of his hand across his mouth. "You about done, bro? I'm sure Ellie has better things to do than watch you act like an asshole."

"Oh, fuck you, *'mano*. You had that coming, and you damn well know it."

A stare down commenced, the two men locked in some sort of silent communication Ellie didn't understand, before Booker's amber gaze landed squarely on her.

Sweet mercy that was some stare. Thousands of butterflies took flight inside her stomach. Ellie searched her ex-husband's face for something, anything familiar to reassure her, but came up empty. This wasn't the young man she'd married. This man was a hardened warrior, cold and fierce and unyielding. He looked almost sinister in black cargo pants—BDU's she thought they were called—and combat boots. A black T-shirt strained against broad shoulders and massive chest. His thick, ropy arms were crossed, drawing her attention to the ink that dotted his biceps.

Her body responded to Booker's blatant masculinity with a warm, tingling sensation low in her belly.

Oh, why did he still have to be so devastatingly handsome?

The angry cut above his eye did nothing to detract from the honeyed tone of his skin. The onyx hair and matching shadow that darkened his cheeks. The ink. The *muscles*.

No, this wasn't the boy she'd known. Booker was a man —fully grown and *intimidating*.

Booker cleared his throat, making her realize she'd been openly ogling him. "Who put that mark on your face? I want a name."

His voice was different, too. Rough. Low and full of gravel. The demand was classic Booker, though. Always the champion.

Ellie diverted her eyes.

It started on her first day of seventh grade. Ellie's dad had left for parts unknown the summer before, never to be seen again. Her mom, saying they needed a fresh start, moved them from Houston to a less-than-desirable area of Austin. The grungy one room apartment they had lived in smelled like stale smoke and gym socks, but it was cheap and the building was close to the small accounting office where her mom answered phones during the day, as well as the restaurant she served drinks in every night of the week.

On Ellie's first day at the new school a group of boys singled her out in the courtyard during lunch. They told her she was pretty. They surrounded her, crowded her into a shadowed corner, despite her protests. When she tried to push past them one of the boys grabbed her by the arm and pulled her close against his scrawny, adolescent body. He was going to kiss her, he'd warned. They were *all* going to kiss her. He threatened to hurt her if she told.

The boy never got the chance to follow through—with the kiss or the threat. Two older, bigger boys came to her rescue. Booker was the taller of her rescuers and had the most beautiful bronzed skin Ellie had ever seen. Booker had given her a reassuring smile before he snagged her aggressor by the back of the neck and threw him to the ground. The boy paled as he tried to protect his face from Booker's fist, to no avail. When blood gushed from the kid's broken nose, Booker leaned down and issued a similar threat about what happened to tattletales.

Brandon effectively dispersed the rest of the group with nothing more than a growl and a glare.

From that day forward, Booker and Brandon had been her friends. Her champions. They were always there, laughing with her, hanging with her, looking out for her. It wasn't until high school that Booker had shown an interest in looking *at* her.

Ellie's heart broke all over again with the memory. They had loved each other once. In another lifetime. Yet there he was. Ready to play savior, regardless of his personal feelings for her—which he made clear the day he'd walked out on their marriage.

Ellie hadn't expected to see him again, but now that he was in front of her ... she would give anything to see even a smidgen of the possessive warmth that used to fill his gaze when he looked at her. A tiny glimmer in recognition of the life they'd almost shared.

Ellie shook the childish notion from her head.

You're pathetic.

Booker had left and never looked back. He hadn't even

called when he received the divorce papers. He hadn't fought for her because she'd given him exactly what he'd wanted. An out.

A profound sadness clawed around in her chest, tearing up old scars, leaving them raw and bloody.

Booker wasn't there out of concern for her. He was there because Brandon tricked him into tagging along. And he'd stay because it had never been in his wheelhouse to walk away from someone in trouble. Even if that someone was his ex-wife.

Ellie rubbed at the pain in her temple. "I can't give you a name, because I don't know."

She should've called the police instead of calling Brandon. As soon as she saw a doctor and got the okay to leave, she'd go to the police station and file a report. Then, she'd find a hotel, because she wasn't going back to her place tonight.

Ellie touched Brandon's arm, hoping he didn't notice how her fingers shook. "Thank you for coming, but you both should go. The doctor will be here any minute to fix me up. I'll be okay."

Brandon's boots didn't budge. He eyed Booker with obvious disappointment. "Yeah. One of us should go." Brandon kept his gaze on Booker as he spoke. "But I'm not budging until I know what happened to land you in here."

Booker folded his arms and settled into his stance. "If you think I'm leaving this room before I get some answers, you're sadly mistaken." To her, he added, "You're not getting off that easy."

The familiar words shivered down her spine.

You're not getting off that easy. Don't you dare, Ellie. Not until I say. Not until—

Booker jerked her arm, gently, but enough to bring her

attention back to him. "Who hurt you?" he demanded, his fingers firm and unyielding against her flesh.

And just like that, newer memories surfaced. In her heart, she knew Booker would never harm her. With the feel of the intruder's brutal hands being the more recent, Ellie reacted to the sensation of the grip, not to the man doing the gripping. She tugged against his hold, fighting back panic. Her face and lungs burned as she twisted her arm at an odd angle. Pain assaulted her already injured shoulder. "Let *go* of me."

Instantly, she was free. She stumbled back a step and sucked in air.

Was there something worse than a nightmare? If so, she was in it.

Booker's palms were raised as if to say, *I don't want any trouble. My hands are right here, unthreatening and un-touching.* While his expression said, *what the actual hell?*

Ellie had the sudden urge to stomp her foot and scream. At the stranger who'd broken into her home. At Booker for pretending to care. At her mom for ... no. Not going there. Not yet. She needed to keep it together. She could fall apart later, when she was alone. Not in front of *him*.

She tucked a non-existent piece of hair behind her ear, a gesture left over from when she wore her hair long instead of the current pixie cut. She slipped her thumb under the delicate chain around her neck and followed it down to the square locket dangling just above the neckline of her shirt. Her mother's locket. It was all Ellie had left of her.

She warmed the jewelry between her fingers. She would get through this. It was just another bump in her pitted-out gravel road.

Blinking back tears, Ellie took a fortifying breath and let the story unfold. "Someone broke into my house this afternoon. I wasn't home at first. I don't know how long..." The strength left her legs and she sank onto the edge of the bed. "He was in the house when I got home."

"He, who?" Booker's tone was less demanding this time.

"I told you, I don't know." Ellie gave them a description of the man and of the destruction to her office. The drawers in her desk had been pulled out, the contents scattered all over the room. The credenza had gotten the same treatment.

"I surprised him when I came in. Before I could run, he was on me." She shuddered, remembering the feel of the intruder's hands around her throat. "He grabbed me and shoved me against the wall. He was clearly angry, but his eyes were desperate, as though if he didn't find what he was looking for there would be hell to pay." Ellie reached up to prod the back of her head. "I fought against his hold, but he slammed my head into the framed photograph I had hanging on the wall."

"What was he looking for?" Booker asked.

"He kept yelling about a flash drive. I tried to tell him I didn't know what he was talking about, but he wasn't interested. He hit me. I remember the impact on my face, but not hitting the floor. By the time I regained awareness, the man was gone."

The bed dipped as Brandon sat beside her, and Ellie leaned into him, grateful for the support. Brandon's arm slid behind her waist as Booker took a knee in front of her. Booker showed her his palms, then slowly lowered them to rest on her knees.

She stared at the hands that had taught her about pleasure. They were large and bruised, each sporting heavy veins and long, capable fingers. Without meaning to, she reached out and smoothed her thumb over his bare ring finger.

He hadn't remarried. She shouldn't be happy about that. Not at all.

Booker breathed her name and she glanced up. "Did he—"

"Ms. King." The doctor strode into the room. "Everything looks— Oh. Hello. I'm Dr. Morris." He offered his hand to Booker, whose brows had plunged upon hearing her maiden name.

She stopped using his last name the minute the divorce papers were filed. Not because she wanted to, but because the constant reminder she'd once been his was more than she could bear.

Booker rocked to his feet and shook the doctor's hand. "Booker Maldano."

The doctor moved on to Brandon. As the men shook Dr. Morris asked, "Friends or family?"

"Friends," Ellie said.

"Family," Booker said at the same time.

Dr. Morris chuckled and turned his attention to her. "Would you like them to wait outside while we go over a few things?"

"No," she shook her head, flabbergasted by Booker's declaration. His hero complex was working overtime tonight. She better be careful not to let his behavior mess with her head. "It's fine. They can stay."

"Very well. I've checked the X-rays. Your ribs and shoulder are bruised, but nothing is broken." He tilted her head and shined a light into her eyes. "No signs of a concussion."

He clicked the penlight off, tucked it into his white coat, and considered her.

"You'll be sore for a few days, but just try to rest as much as you can." He held up a tiny paper cup. "These will help with the pain as well as help you get some sleep. If these gentlemen are here to drive you home, you can take them now. Otherwise—"

"She has a ride," Booker said. "Take them."

As though his word were law, the doctor handed Ellie the cup. He went to the sink to fill a cup of water and brought it back to her. She sent Mr. Bossy Pants a look to let him know she swallowed the pills because she wanted to—for the pain—not because Booker had demanded she do so.

"By tomorrow, an over-the-counter pain medication should be enough to manage the soreness. If not, call your regular doctor for a prescription." The doctor eyed the other men, one brow cocked. "Either of you boys need a doctor?"

After the simultaneous *we're good*'s Ellie thanked the doctor and watched as Brandon and Booker took turns doing the same. As soon as the doctor left, Brandon turned to her.

"Until we figure this out, you can't go home."

"Agreed," Booker said. "The guy might decide to come back. We still have the cottage Ketcher was using, right?"

Brandon nodded. "Yeah."

"I'll take her there and stay with her while you figure out—"

"Whoa." Ellie put on the brakes. She wasn't going anywhere alone with Booker. "Hold up, you two. The first thing I need to do is file a police report. I should've done that before I came here, but I wasn't exactly thinking clearly."

Booker checked his watch. "And in about fifteen minutes you won't be thinking at all, so why don't you relax, let the pain medication do its job, and let us do ours."

Right. Because she was a job to him. Good to know.

"I'll call a buddy of mine at the department," Brandon

offered. "I'll have him meet me at Ellie's house so he can document the scene. You said the guy asked about a flash drive. Why would he believe you had something like that?"

Her head throbbed. "I don't know. He had to have the wrong house. I don't have...the only time..." Oh God. The courier.

But, that couldn't be right. She received the same drive once a week from her boss. He sent audio files for her to transcribe. When she was finished she saved the transcriptions on the same drive and sent it back to his secretary. Week after week, for the last eight years.

Booker took her elbow. "What is it?"

"Probably nothing. A coincidence." She explained how she received work from her boss.

"Seems archaic," Booker mused. "Wouldn't a direct connection to the server be more efficient?"

Ellie wasn't going to get into the reasons why she hadn't made upgrading the technology at her house a priority. "We all work with what we've got."

"Where is the drive that was delivered today?" Brandon asked.

"Locked in the glove compartment of my car. The courier caught me on the way out, and when my car ... well, it doesn't matter. I didn't want to leave the envelope out in the open so I locked it up. By the time I got home, I'd forgotten all about it."

Brandon headed toward the door. "Mind if we take a look?"

Ellie shrugged. "If you don't mind being bored to tears with corporate legal mumbo jumbo, be my guest. I guarantee none of the files my boss sends to me are worth breaking and entering and assault charges."

3

Ellie led them to an economy car parked in the visitor's lot. The thing was a POS. A rust bucket on wheels.

"You actually drive this thing?" Booker scanned the surrounding area as Ellie unlocked the passenger door. Twenty-four hours ago, Regan had been snatched from the adjoining lot. Booker had seen the video feed. The helplessness of seeing Regan being shoved into the trunk of a car was still too fresh in his mind.

"I don't do a lot of driving. It usually gets me from point A to point B, which is all I care about."

Booker wanted to question her about why she didn't drive much, but Ellie had already climbed into the car and was working the lock on the glove compartment.

Booker caged her in, resting one arm against the doorframe, the other against the edge of the open door. He should probably give her some space, but until he knew what was going on he had no intention of backing off.

Brandon levered his ass onto the hood on the other side of the door, watching Booker's six while Booker focused on Ellie.

Just like old times.

Only it wasn't. Everything was different now. He wasn't the same man. He and Ellie weren't a couple. Hell, they weren't even friends.

He wanted to be annoyed that she and Brandon had maintained their friendship without his knowledge, but he couldn't summon the energy. He was too busy basking in the perverse pleasure he felt over the fact she called a friend—Brandon—instead of another man. A romantic partner. The idea of some other bastard taking care of his wife made him mental.

Welcome to my twelve years of insanity.

What kind of sick fuck was he that he couldn't think of her in any other way than as his wife? He inked the divorce papers. He moved his stuff. He respected her wish to be free of him and had gone on with his life. He even took a woman to bed, although not often. The guilt after each encounter chipped away at his soul.

He'd given fucking *vows*, for Christ's sake. A man didn't forget something like that no matter how long he lived. Or existed, in his case, since he could hardly call what he did as living. Whatever. Semantics.

Booker swiped a hand down his face.

It didn't take a rocket scientist to understand he had some unresolved issues. Those issues were his burden to bear. The wisest course of action would be to forget about the past and focus on the tasks at hand. Determine the source of the threat. Eliminate it. Go home. Sleep for a month. Bam.

The glove compartment fell open and Ellie pulled out a manila envelope with her name scrawled across the front. Tearing open one end, she peered inside with a frown. "That's strange."

"What?" Booker leaned down and caught a whiff of her scent. She smelled like summer on the beach. Coconut and some kind of fruit. He'd never craved a piña colada more in his life. He'd have to keep a lid on that shit. Ellie needed his protection, not his dick. But damn if the traitor didn't perk behind his fly anyway.

"There are two drives."

"And that's unusual?"

She dumped the contents into her palm and inspected each one. "I've been off work quiet a bit lately, but they've never sent two before, so I'd say yes."

Brandon launched himself off the car's hood. "Let's go inside and find Noah. Let him take a quick look before we decide what to do next."

A fine idea, except the last time Booker had seen their computer expert in the waiting room, the guy had been turbo sucking his way to the bottom of a flask.

Booker held out his palm to Ellie. "Let me have those." Once she dropped the stick-shaped devices into his hand, he backed away to give her room to get out of the vehicle. "We'll use one of Noah's laptops and take a look ourselves."

Ellie reached into the backseat and pulled out a duffel bag. She locked the car door and shoved it shut. Her movements were slow and uncoordinated. Booker lifted her chin and checked her eyes. Heavy eyelids and small pupils. The painkillers were kicking in. "You doing okay?"

She jerked her chin from his grip. "What do you think?"

Booker eyed the duffel. He'd bet his left nut she had clothes and probably some toiletries in there. "You weren't planning to go home tonight, were you? Where were you going to go?"

"To a hotel for a couple of days." She readjusted the strap on her shoulder. "Do you really believe there's something on the drives worth hurting me over? I work for Jennings, Bradford & Mosley. They aren't criminal attorneys. Owen, my boss, practices corporate law."

"Plenty of crooked corporations out there," Booker said. "It stands to reason they would hire crooked attorneys."

"Owen Jennings is big shit in Austin," Brandon said as he flanked Ellie's left and started back toward the entrance to the ER. "Word is he's throwing his hat into the political arena."

Ellie nodded. "He mentioned plans to run for mayor. And he doesn't want to stop there. Ultimately, he plans to run for senate."

Booker instantly hated big shit Owen who apparently had no problem sharing his personal aspirations with Booker's wife.

Ex-wife. Christ. He was a mess.

And what kind of name was *Owen*? Sounded like a name for a missionary position, tighty-whitey wearing motherfucker. How exactly was Ellie involved with the man? Booker's vision went a little wonky thinking about Ellie as the underside of Owen's missionary so he forced the vision out of his brain before it stuck.

Booker fell in step on Ellie's right. "A bid for office is gonna take money. Greed is a powerful motivator for engaging in illegal activity. Are you sleeping with him?"

Not very smooth, but Booker had to know.

Ellie pressed the heel of her palm against one eye. "I so don't need this right now. What the hell am I supposed to do if there's something illegal on those drives? And if there is, why would Owen send them to me?"

Booker heard the car before he saw it. Behind them an engine revved. Tires squealed against the pavement. He jerked around and a set of headlights burst on, momentarily blinding him.

"Fuck! Look out!" Training and instinct took over. Booker snagged Ellie around the waist and pulled her back against his chest. Using all of his strength, he launched them between two cars, out of the way of the SUV that seemed determined to mow them down.

"Brandon?" he yelled as he scanned the parking lot. Fuck. Had the guy been hit?

A groan. Then, "I'm good. You guys okay?"

Booker released Ellie and spun her to face him before giving her a once over. She looked dazed, but otherwise uninjured. "We're good. What the fuck was that?"

Brandon stood a few cars away and dusted himself off. "A coincidence?"

Booker caught sight of red taillights before the SUV jacked a u-ey. Two men burst from the backseat and hit the ground running.

Booker crouched behind a car, tugging Ellie down with him. "Does a coincidence come back for seconds?" He held up two fingers, using them to point in the direction of the men headed toward them. "Incoming."

He was unarmed, damn it. They'd never make it to the safety of the ER before either the men or the truck got to them. "Got any bright ideas?"

Brandon cursed and pulled out his cell and his keys. He put the phone to his ear and tossed him the keys. "I'll handle this shit. My truck is four rows over. Take it and get her the fuck out of here, man."

Booker didn't hesitate. He tightened his grip on Ellie's hand and made a break for Brandon's truck.

"Wait!" She dug her heels into the pavement. "We can't leave Brandon."

"We can and we will. Brandon can take care of himself."
Plus, there was a waiting room full of backup Booker
suspected were already on the way. "Use your feet, Ellie, or
I'll toss you over my fucking shoulder. Either way, we're out
of here."

Thank God she stopped fighting. Behind them, tires
screeched and the distinct *pop pop* of shots being fired rang
out. A car window on Booker's left exploded.

Ellie screamed. "Brandon!"

He jerked Ellie in front of him, eliminating her as a
target. "They're not shooting at him."

Booker picked up the pace, pressing his hand against
her lower back to guide her. With the other he used the
remote to disengage the door locks on the truck.

Sirens blared in the distance. An incoming ambulance.

Within seconds Booker threw open the passenger side
door of the truck and all but tossed Ellie into the seat.
"Buckle up, then keep your head down."

He didn't wait for her to comply. He slammed the door.
A quick glance over his shoulder verified the call Brandon
made had brought Roman and Sully running. Behind them
a uniformed cop burst through the doors, weapon drawn
and ready for action.

Booker jumped into the vehicle. He kept the lights off as
he surged out of the parking spot. He switched gears,
cranked the wheel, and hauled ass out of the parking lot. He
took a right, planning to head for the highway and from
there, the lake cottage where he and the guys had been
bunking with Ketcher.

He checked the rear view in time to see the SUV
barreling toward the exit.

"Shit. Hang on."

He slammed on the brakes and made a sharp left onto a side street. Guided by memory, he wound through the neighborhood, choosing streets at random until he was sure they weren't being followed. Only then did he allow himself to glance over at Ellie. She'd been far too quiet for his liking. For good reason, it seemed. Bent forward in the seat with her cheek resting against her knee, Ellie's glassy stare met his.

Hello, painkillers. The woman was high as a kite.

"Are you hurt?"

"My ... my fingers feel weird." As if to demonstrate, Ellie sat up and showed him her hand. She wiggled her digits. His smile died before it got started.

No, damn it. He would not be charmed.

Booker swore under his breath. For twelve long years he'd been perfectly fine living in ignorance of her life, keeping his emotions locked down tight. Within seconds, *seconds*, she had stolen that ignorance from him.

He knew things now. Current, not-from-memory, things. Her tropical scent. That she had new and adorable little crinkles around her eyes. That her breasts looked fucking amazing under that tank top.

It wasn't so much the new knowledge of her that ruffled his feathers. Oh no. His problem was that she made him *feel*. Back in the ER, all the hurt and anger had come rushing back to mingle with a sense of confusion and relief at seeing her again, followed quickly by irritation and yes, arousal. He'd been hard as a fucking rock from the moment she had opened her mouth to speak. There was another, more troublesome, emotion lurking around in his chest, but it could just stay there, locked up tight behind his ribs.

The way he saw it he had two choices. Be a prick so she

would stop being so damn cute, or spank her ass bright red for turning him into an emotional volcano. He doubted she'd appreciate being tossed over his lap.

"Do you have a cell phone?" he asked.

"Yep. It's in my bag."

"Give it to me."

"What do you—"

"You can argue later, but right now I need you to give me the goddamn phone."

Booker lowered the window as she reached into her bag and pulled out the device.

"Here."

"Thank you." He took the phone and in one fluid motion, tossed it from the vehicle.

"Hey! What the hell?"

"Someone just tried to run you down. They could've found you by tracking your phone."

"You're making assumptions." She tilted her head to rest against the window and she closed her eyes. "How do you know it was me they were trying to run over? Maybe they were after you. Maybe it was the same person who cracked your head open?"

A good theory, with one fatal flaw. "Not possible."

She did have a point, though. He and the guys had gone head-to-head with members of the Cuban cartel and won. He'd be a fool not to consider the possibility of retaliation.

"Why not?" Her words ran together. She was fading fast.

"Because the guy who clocked me is dead."

The sound of her sharp inhale filled the truck. "Did you kill him?"

Booker's head throbbed. Now was not the time for a conversation about his life and the things he'd done.

"Get some rest, Ellie."

He hit the expressway and floored the gas, wanting to put as much space as possible between them and Austin as possible. Or maybe just them.

4

Daylight arrived gracefully over the lake.

Ellie had a perfect view of the show from the couch. Curled up on one end, she toyed with the locket around her neck. The night sky awoke with gradient tones of purple and pink. Within minutes, hues of purple melted into blue, pink into orange and gold until the lake glittered like it was covered in diamonds.

Beautiful. I could live here forever.

Wherever *here* was.

She'd come out of her medicated nap to find herself alone in a bedroom she didn't recognize. She'd been stretched out on the bed on top of the comforter with a throw blanket covering her legs. Her duffel bag was perched on a chair in the corner. Still dressed in the clothes she'd worn to the hospital, Ellie changed into her usual sleep attire of yoga shorts and a sports bra and crawled back into the bed, hoping for more sleep.

When sleep refused to come, she went in search of Booker, only to realize she hadn't just been alone in the bedroom. The cottage was empty. She might've gotten nervous if Brandon's truck hadn't still been parked beyond the dilapidated porch out front.

The cottage was small, so it didn't take long to snoop around. There were two bedrooms and a living area. The bathroom was on the other side of the large kitchen. There were dirty dishes in the sink, and a laptop and computer monitor on the kitchen table. The latter appeared to be video feed of the exterior of the cottage and what she assumed was the surrounding area. The place held the faint scent of stale fish and lake water. She surmised she was in the cottage Booker had mentioned, but that's where the knowledge of her location ended.

Booker.

God. He could've at least had the decency to add some body fat over the years instead of all those...those *muscles.*

Her body hadn't fared quite so well. Her curves had thinned to within an inch of being dainty—a look her five-feet-six frame couldn't pull off as healthy. For the last eight years, she'd been her mom's full time caregiver. With her focus on her mom, she hadn't done a great job taking care of herself. She lost enough weight over the years to make her hipbones visible. Her stomach wasn't ripped, more ... soft and flat. She'd gone down one whole bra cup size, which she didn't necessarily mind since it meant her breasts were perkier than before. Not that anyone ever saw them. The only decision Ellie had consciously made about her appearance involved her hair. She had her long waves cut into a short pixie to save time and energy.

She didn't look horrible. Nothing a few more cheeseburgers and calorie-laden meals wouldn't take care of.

Low maintenance had been her self-proclaimed motto for herself while her mother had been sick.

Ellie winced as she ran a hand over her rib cage; lest she

forget about the other ways her body hadn't improved. The discoloration of the bruise covering the left side of her torso had turned into a sickly purple. The bruise matched the one on her thigh.

Could Owen have been responsible for her attack? The trouble at the hospital?

She slid the locket back and forth on the chain.

If he was, the bigger question became … why?

Booker thought she and Owen—Ellie almost gagged. No and no. She and Owen weren't involved—had never *been* involved. Not romantically anyway.

Owen was her boss. He'd been kind after her mom died. Owen wasn't an estate attorney, so when he offered to help her navigate the legalities surrounding her mom's estate at no charge, Ellie had been touched by the sentiment. She should've seen his support for what it was. A strategic play to have her indebted to him.

Owen overestimated her affection. She overestimated Owen's sanity.

I always get what I want, Elizabeth. Darling. There's no need to resist. I know you want me as much as I want you.

She didn't want him, but she needed her job. She indulged Owen with occasional dinners, drinks, and phone calls, but she shut him down flat whenever he tried to get physical. With her focus on caring for her mom 24/7, Ellie hadn't been with a man in more years than she wanted to count. She wasn't going to end her drought with a pompous ass like Owen Jennings.

Owen hadn't given up. If anything, the more she resisted, the more aggressive he'd become. Worried Owen would stop taking no for an answer, she begged off his invitations and started looking for a new job.

Needing to move, Ellie slid from the loveseat and walked

to the back door. Glittery dew covered the trees, making them sparkle in the morning light. A fine mist hovered close to the ground, giving the yard a tranquil, almost ethereal quality.

The peacefulness of it beckoned her. After the chaos of the last year, she wanted—no, *needed*—to be a part of it. To breathe it in. To create a memory she could take with her and recall long after she left this place.

She opened the door and stepped into the spacious screened-in porch. Her body immediately revolted with a head-to-toe shiver-burst when the morning chill hit her skin. She should've put a shirt on over her sports bra before going out. And maybe some pants to cover her legs, but damn. The chill invigorated her.

The painted concrete floor was slick with dew. Cautiously, she padded over to the screen wall. She leaned into the morning and drew in a breath. Crisp air filled her lungs. Somewhere in the distance, a bird chirped a cheerful good morning.

She had died and gone to heaven.

"What're you doing out here?"

Ellie whirled around. Booker leaned in the doorway, holding a coffee mug in each hand. He'd traded his military pants for jeans and nothing else. Holy sexy tattoo, Booker's left pec sported ink that hadn't been there the last time she'd seen his bare chest. An eagle done in black. Its talons were extended, the wings spread. It appeared to be coming in for a landing over his heart. One wing spanned his shoulder. There were single feathers trailing down and around his biceps, as if the eagle had shed them.

She couldn't take her eyes off all that glorious skin. His torso was solid from the bulk of his shoulders to his corrugated abs. Built as he was, Booker should never, ever wear a shirt.

Shirt. Damn it, he wasn't the only one not wearing one.

Snapping out of her tattoo and muscle trance, Ellie slapped her arms over her middle. Too late. Booker's lazy smile vanished as his gaze dipped down. A rush of Spanish tumbled from his lips. He dropped the mugs. They fell to the floor with a fractured *clank* as he stormed toward her.

Okay, so she'd missed a few meals during her mom's eight-year illness, but she didn't look *that* bad.

Ellie stumbled back, back, back, matching his forward movement step for step until she found herself wedged against the far corner of the porch with Booker looming over her. Despite the chill, her body heated.

"W-what are you doing?"

"You said you weren't hurt." Booker reached out, his hand hovering next to her cheek as though wanting to touch, but unsure if he should. When they'd been together he wouldn't have thought twice about taking what he wanted from her. And she wouldn't have thought twice about letting him.

Her stomach dropped and rolled as the muscles in her core clenched. It had been so long since she'd been touched with any semblance of tenderness, Ellie suddenly felt starved for the feeling.

Please. Touch me.

She missed him, damn it. She could deny it later, when her emotions weren't raw, but God, the concern crinkling his beautiful eyes right now ... it was too much.

Ellie's hand shook as she cupped his knuckles. Holding him in place, she leaned in to his touch. Her eyelids fluttered closed with the contact.

Warm. Calloused. Perfect.

If she thought she was in heaven before, Booker's touch had upgraded her to the VIP section. She didn't move. Didn't blink. Didn't breathe. She just ... *felt.*

Booker's thumb brushed her cheek. "Did he do this?"

Despite the caress, his tone had bite. Ellie came back to earth in a sudden crash. She opened her eyes and glanced up into the face of a stranger. All hard-edged and ready for battle.

What would it be like to wrap herself around him now? To channel all that menace into something more pleasurable?

Keep dreaming. He left you, remember?

Yeah. She remembered.

Ellie tilted her head away from his hand and ignored the deepening crease between his brows. Booker reacted to the bruises because he was a decent guy who wouldn't want to see anyone hurt. She could've been anyone and his reaction would've been the same. He was a champion. That's why he joined the military. And it was why he was helping her now.

She was a job.

"If you're asking whether the guy who broke into my house gave me these bruises, then yes. Although the one on my face was the only direct hit. The others came from the subsequent fall."

Using her palms, Ellie nudged Booker's chest, hoping he would take the hint and give her some breathing room. He backed off with a grunt of disapproval.

She shivered with the loss of his heat.

"Damn it. Come on." Booker grabbed her hand and tugged her toward the door. He took two steps before he turned to look at her. Ellie had no idea what that scowl meant. It wasn't her fault she was bruised.

He released her hand.

"*Vas a acabar conmigo*," he said to the ceiling. Before she took another breath he bent down, hooked an arm behind her knees, and lifted her into his arms.

HONEST TO GOD, Booker had planned for a fresh start with Ellie this morning. Beyond the shock of seeing her again and the trouble she was potentially in, he was determined to start over. This time, his emotions wouldn't get the better of him. He'd be calm—they would talk. He'd be cool—he would absolutely *not* think about seeing her tight little body naked. He'd be collected—and finally get some answers.

A perfectly executable plan blown to shit the minute he laid eyes on those bruises. Calm, cool, and collected flew the fucking coop, leaving him with a whole mess of pissed off and a fiery need to make someone pay for marring her beautiful skin.

"What do you think you're doing?" She struggled against him. "Put me down."

Not if his life depended on it. Not yet. "There are pieces of broken coffee mug all over the porch. I don't want you to get cut." Maybe it was the broken shards of ceramic on the concrete. Maybe he needed reassurance that she was okay. Whatever the reason, it felt too good to have her in his arms again.

Where she belonged.

Ellie huffed in a sexy little protest, but she stopped squirming. And then she did the most amazing thing. She looped an arm around him, her fingers dancing along the back of his neck on their way to his shoulder. Her gaze locked onto his tattoo and fuck him, she wet her lips. "And I suppose your feet are made of iron?"

His feet? No. But if she kept that shit up his cock would make a fine simulation.

"I was smart enough to put on shoes before stepping out onto the cold porch." And pants. Another item she'd forgotten that he was having a hard time being annoyed about when it meant he had an unobstructed view of her long legs.

"How was I supposed to know your morning ritual included sacrifices to the coffee gods? I hope one of those mugs was for me. I'd hate to get on the wrong side of that particular deity so soon after my arrival."

Booker rolled his eyes, but her joke eased the tension in his chest. Gave him the strength to set her back on her feet once they reached the door.

"Go put on some clothes," he said, ushering her inside. Those bruises were making him twitchy as hell. "I'll pour you a fresh sacrifice and then we're going to talk."

Ellie disappeared into the bedroom. Booker grabbed a broom and dustpan and headed back outside. By the time he'd cleaned and disposed of the mess, Ellie sat at the kitchen table waiting for him. Her feet were still bare, but she added a pair of jeans and another tank top. Pink, this time. Her fingers were laced together in her lap. Her thumb was busy circling the opposite palm, a clear sign she was nervous. She'd picked up the habit when they were kids.

Booker pulled on a T-shirt and filled the last two coffee mugs from the cabinet. He left his black. To Ellie's he added a healthy amount of cream and a splash of the maple syrup Roman had put in the fridge for the frozen waffles the guy consumed by the dozen.

He crossed to the table and set the mug down in front of her. He'd gone out before daybreak to check the perimeter alarms he and Roman had set in preparation for Ketcher's stay at the cottage. While out, he called Brandon, who had already thought about the possible Cuban connection to last night's shit storm. The SUV and the men had gotten away, but Brandon was looking into it. In the meantime, Booker needed to work the other angle.

"Owen," he ground out, hating the taste of the asshole's name. "Start talking."

Ellie wrapped her hands around the mug. "You first. What did you mean when you said I was going to be the death of you?"

"What?"

"Before you picked me up on the porch, you basically said I was going to be the death of you. Why?"

Because this will end, and I don't know how I'll survive letting you go again.

"When did you learn Spanish?"

She smiled a little, like she knew he was deflecting but wouldn't press the issue. Good thing, since he had no interest in cracking his chest for her inspection.

"I decided to take classes right before we got married." She winced at the word *married*, as though being attached to him had been less than desirable. "I wanted it to be a surprise. Then, when you decided to leave..." She shrugged. "I needed something to do that first year."

When he *decided* to leave? She thought he *wanted* to be apart from her? Fuck that. Her choice of phrase crawled all over him, like an army of hungry fire ants.

He wasn't the one who left.

"Other than file divorce papers, you mean?"

44

5

And so it begins.

"That didn't take long," Ellie murmured and took a sip of coffee, surprised to find the familiar maple flavor on her tongue. He remembered how she took her coffee. What other surprises did this man have in store for her?

She was almost afraid to find out.

"Took twelve fucking years. Maybe you want to take another stab at that memory, Ells. Time seems to have skewed the chain of events for you."

There was nothing wrong with her memory. "I remember everything."

"Except the part about who left who."

They hadn't spoken since before the divorce, so this conversation seemed inevitable. He wanted to do this now? Fine. Best they get it done and out of the way if they were going to be around each other for any length of time.

She jabbed a finger at him. "You said you couldn't do it anymore."

He scoffed. "What are you talking about?"

"Now who doesn't remember? The last time you called

me from overseas, you said you couldn't do it anymore. That you were done. What did you expect me to do? Stay with a man who didn't want me?"

"Didn't want..." His brows scrunched together as if searching for the memory. "I didn't mean our marriage. How could you even *think* that? I meant I couldn't fight with you anymore. I was thousands of miles away fighting a different kind of war. I couldn't stand to battle with you as well. For fuck's sake, Ellie. I pledged my life to you. I gave you my word that you were it for me."

"Men say things all the time that they don't mean."

"Not this man," he growled.

"Oh really? And the promise to always be by my side? What about that?" Ellie took a breath. "You know how important having a family was to me. I spent my childhood alone, the only daughter of a single mom who worked more than she was home. There were times I thought the quiet would drive me insane. I didn't have anyone to talk to. And then you came into my life. You and your big, close family. You showed me what it meant to have people who paid attention to what was going on in your life. People who cared whether you ate or did your homework. People who cared if you were safe."

Don't cry. Don't cry. Do. Not. Cry.

"That's all I ever wanted. A family I could call my own. You. A houseful of children. I wanted to love and be loved. I didn't want to be alone in the world."

Ellie choked on those last words and the anger seeped out of her in a rush. Her mom was gone. She *was* alone.

"I would've given you that. I would've given you *everything*."

It was her turn to scoff. "Everything except you."

"That's bullshit. You had me lock, stock, and fucking barrel. How could you even doubt that?"

"Oh, please. You left before the ink was even dry on our marriage license!" The words burst loudly from her lips, petulant as a spoiled child. "And I was alone. *Again*."

His deployment hadn't just broken her heart, it had shattered her innocence. Suddenly, she wasn't a kid anymore. She was an eighteen-year-old married adult with married adult problems and responsibilities. She wasn't free to dream about who and what she might become. She was a military wife without a husband at home, barely old enough to handle paying the bills, let alone the rioting emotions inside her.

"To serve my country!" he shouted back. "The same country that welcomed my grandparents from Spain years ago. To serve in honor of the opportunity given to my family. To do my part to keep you and the people I love safe. It wasn't as though I had tons of job opportunities and college wasn't..." His lips clamped into a thin line. "You know my grades weren't the best." His chest rose and fell in a steady rhythm. "I had a family, a *wife*, to consider. I did what I thought was best."

"You made that decision without discussing it with me. The *wife* you say you were so concerned about."

That had hurt most of all. He'd shut her out of the most important decision of his life. He hadn't respected her enough to ask for her opinion. Had he expected her to live unsure of when the next bomb would be dropped? Where was the partnership in that?

His cruel laughter fell over her like a sudden snowfall. "Is that what you tell yourself when you're alone at night? Is that how you justify ending our marriage before we even had a chance to get started?" He made a noise of disgust. "My plan to become a Marine was never a secret."

"We talked in hypotheticals, Booker. What ifs. Never once did you actually say you were going to join the Marines. Not even on the day you enlisted." She couldn't keep the resentment from her voice. "You and Brandon made the decision to go together, without so much as a hint as to where you were going. You made a decision that also affected my life, without giving me a say. What was I supposed to do with that?"

"You were supposed to be there for me. To support my decision. The second," Booker slammed his fist against the table, "the *fucking second* things didn't go the way you imagined, you bailed."

Ellie stared down at her hands, blinking furiously to keep the tears at bay. His choice to join the military had been an honorable one. His heart had been in the right place, but his execution had sucked. And yes, she had been the one to instigate the divorce. But it took two to tango, didn't it?

"And you let me."

God, they had been so young. It hadn't taken her long to realize her mistake, but by then—

An alarm rang out, loud and insistent. Booker surged to his feet so fast his chair toppled over. He grabbed the edge of the computer monitor and turned it so he could see the display.

"Son of a bitch." He started pulling wires.

Ellie jumped to her feet. "What is it?"

He tapped a finger against one of the live feed images on the screen a second before the screen went dark. "Company. We gotta go."

"I'll grab my bag."

48

"No time." He snatched up the laptop and a large duffel bag, then grabbed her arm. He headed toward the door.

"I'm not wearing shoes!"

He spun, dropped, and shoved his shoulder into her uninjured side. A strong arm braced her legs as he surged back to his full height.

The breath whooshed from her lungs. Feeling the urgency in his muscular frame, Ellie didn't protest being carried like a sack of potatoes. Nor did she protest being unceremoniously dumped onto the passenger seat of the truck. He slammed the door and jogged around the front of the vehicle to the other side.

"Buckle up," he barked as he dropped into the driver's seat. He shoved the laptop between the seat and the center console before starting the engine.

"Sir, yes, sir," she mumbled.

Ellie thought she saw his lips twitch as he slammed the truck into gear and hit the gas.

BOOKER AVOIDED USING THE DRIVEWAY. He drove around the side of the house, then cut across the back yard. He had plotted an escape route the first night he'd been at the cottage—the night Ketcher had arrived, wounded and burning up with fever.

Brandon had selected the perfect spot for Ketcher to lay low while he healed from an injury sustained during the mission that ended with the death of the Cuban drug lord. Rented under an untraceable alias—thanks to Brandon's younger brother Alec—the property was fairly large and wooded on two sides, with the lake bordering the back. Booker and Roman had secured the perimeter. Sully and

49

Adam had placed underground sensors at the head of the single road leading to the place, as well as at the top of the driveway...which in itself was a quarter of a mile long.

Once security was in place, Booker had mapped an alternate route to the main road in the event one of Ketcher's enemies came calling. He hadn't actually expected to use it, though.

Booker followed the shoreline, staying as far away from the edge of the lake as possible. The ground close to the water was soft. The truck would leave ruts noticeable enough to be followed.

The truck bounced and trembled as Booker cut between the trees and hit the rougher ground of the woods.

Out of the corner of his eye he saw Ellie grab the *oh shit* bar to steady herself. She hadn't said a word since he put her in the truck, which suited him just fine. The silence gave him the opportunity to regroup.

Their fight had made his chest burn. Her accusation had flayed him open, left his insides exposed.

She thought he hadn't wanted her. That she hadn't been the reason for every breath he took. That she hadn't been the light that kept his world from utter darkness.

He'd talked to her about the Marines. He'd been up front about his desire to join. Of course he had.

Hadn't he?

His ass left the seat as the truck rolled over a stump. Ellie grunted and raised her free arm, bracing herself against the ceiling of the cab.

Fuck. Whatever she believed, however wrong she'd been about his feelings for her, he couldn't think about it now. He had other, more pressing, problems.

Doing his best to ignore his passenger, Booker pulled out his cell phone and called Brandon.

"It's early, Spaniard," Brandon quipped in way of greeting, his voice rough with sleep.

"Sorry to interrupt your beauty sleep. A black SUV just triggered the underground sensor at the main road."

"Same one from last night?"

"I'd say that's a safe assumption."

"Where are you?"

"On the move. We pulled out when the alarm sounded."

Brandon went quiet for a minute. Then, "Are you thinking what I'm thinking?"

"That last night wasn't about Ellie? Yeah." He glanced over to find Ellie sporting an I-told-you-so smirk. "I was informed of the possibility."

He returned his focus to the terrain and to getting them the hell out of there. "It makes sense. Whoever broke into her house left her alive." Bile rose in his throat as he realized how easily the fucker could've killed her. "Why do that, then try to run her over in the parking lot? It doesn't make sense. And while the contents of the flash drives are still an unknown, I believe the incidents are unrelated. There is nothing to tie Ellie to the cottage."

"Maybe they tracked her cell phone."

"Who do you think you're talking to, '*mano*? I tossed her phone out the window last night as we were leaving the parking lot."

"But not your phone. You think the cartel tracked you?"

"Unlikely." Even if it were possible—and Booker highly doubted it—the cartel wouldn't have had time to identify the other players in Ketcher's rescue mission yesterday. "My guess is they somehow linked the cottage to Ketcher."

"How? Alec wouldn't have left a trail. He's better than that."

Booker scrubbed a hand over his mouth. He had too

51

many questions and not enough answers. "I have no idea, but they found Regan. She hadn't spoken to Ketch in four years. If they figured out the connection between Ketch and Regan because of the way they looked at each other in a photograph taken years ago in a war zone, they can find their way to a cottage."

There was something about the theory that didn't set well, but it was the only thing that made sense. Whoever wanted the information Ellie supposedly had couldn't have tracked her to the lake. Unless...

Booker slammed on the brakes. The truck came to a violent stop. His gaze hit the rearview to make sure they didn't have a tail.

"Is it possible to track a flash drive?" He didn't wait for Brandon's answer. He'd seen crazier things than someone implanting a tracking device on a drive housing important files. He jerked the laptop from where it was stored. He brought his shoulder up, using it to hold the phone against his cheek so he'd have both hands free. He balanced the laptop against the steering wheel the best he could and raised the screen. He extended his leg and lifted his hip. The laptop tumbled when he tried to reach into his pocket to retrieve the flash drives Ellie had given him.

On the cell, Brandon's voice was muffled, apparently posing Booker's question to someone else.

Beside him Ellie shifted. "Give me that," she snapped. She took the laptop and settled it against her thighs.

Booker didn't argue. "Power it up."

The glare she sent him said his demand hadn't earned him any favors. The plan formulating in his head probably wouldn't either.

She held his stare, her expression full of piss and vinegar as she deliberately punched the power button.

His dick went hard in an instant.

Awesome. Just what he needed. To be turned on by her sass.

He jammed his hand into his pocket and wrapped his fingers around the drives. He gave his traitorous cock a shove on the retreat to keep from getting pinched when he lowered back to the seat.

Doing his best to ignore what was going on down south he passed her the drives. "Copy the entire contents of these onto the laptop. Be quick about it. We need to keep moving."

He checked the rearview. Nothing but trees.

She snatched them from his hand. "You've become a real ass, you know that? Would it kill you to say please?"

No, baby, it wouldn't, but I like it better when you say it.

Christ. Where the hell had that come from?

"Alec says it's possible to implant a tracking device on just about anything." Brandon's voice rang loud and clear in Booker's ear, distracting him from his own personal hell. "Please tell me you have a way to copy the files and ditch the drives. Better safe than sorry."

"Already on it."

Booker shoved open the door. Palm up, he held his hand out to Ellie. He kept his gaze glued to their surroundings and waited until he felt the weight of the devices being dropped into his palm. Or slapped. Whatever. Once he had them he was out of the truck and on his knees, burying the drives in the dirt.

"Can Alec ping my exact location within the next twenty seconds?" He brushed off his hands on his pants and stood over the buried drives, waiting. He didn't want to hang around any longer than absolutely necessary.

There was more shuffling on the line. "Yep. Hang on. There. He's got you."

"Make note of the coordinates in case we need to recover the drives, although I don't know how good they'll be after being in the wet ground. And we should let the guys know this location has been compromised."

"By 'we' you mean me?"

"Obviously."

Brandon laughed. "Yeah, sure, dickhead. I'll handle it."

"One of the guys should stay with Ketcher, just in case. And would you go over to *Abuelita's* and keep an eye on things until we know what's going on?" Booker's grandmother loved Brandon. Considered him part of the family. More importantly, Brandon's appearance wouldn't cause suspicion. Booker didn't want to worry them if there was no cause. Right now, he had no idea if there was cause or not.

"And what are you going to do?"

Get as far away from Texas as he could. There was only one place they could go where he could keep Ellie safe while he figured out what the hell was going on.

"Sorry, man, but it looks like I'm going to need your truck a while longer. I'm going home, and I'm taking Ellie with me."

6

Ellie thought they would continue the discussion they'd been forced to leave unfinished, but she was sadly mistaken. Booker didn't show any interest in discussing ... well, anything. Not even where they were going except for a grumbled "Montana."

She hadn't asked any more questions.

Two hours into the mystery road trip of silence they stopped at a truck stop, where Booker bought her a pair of flip flops for her bare feet, and a hot meal in the attached restaurant. Where they ate in more silence.

Six hours into the trip they stopped for gas. Using one and two syllable words to communicate, Booker escorted her to the restroom, waited outside the door for her to finish, and then escorted her back to the truck.

As though she were a child.

The ten-hour mark found them inside a discount store, where Booker upped his syllable count to insist she put whatever she needed into the cart—clothes, toiletries, shoes, snacks, whatever. Since her wallet was in the duffel bag back at the cottage, she didn't have much choice but to allow him to pay for the toothbrush and toothpaste, shampoo, conditioner, deodorant, a pair of sleep shorts, a four-pack of ribbed cotton tank tops in various colors, and a six-pack of boy short style panties. His jaw had tightened as she'd thrown the last item into the cart. Well, to hell with him. She would pay back every cent the minute she had access to her bank account.

By the time they rolled into a motel parking lot outside of Pueblo, Colorado, Ellie's nerves were shot. Thirteen hours of uncomfortable silence and side glances were more than she could take. She had no idea what was going on in that head of his, and right now, she didn't give a damn.

She wanted out of the truck. She wanted a hot shower and a comfortable bed. Most of all, she wanted away from him.

Booker stopped in front of a door marked *Office* and let the truck idle. With his hand on the door handle he turned to her. "Don't move."

She was going to fucking choke him.

She had no money. No mode of transport other than him, and she was umpteen miles away from home. She was totally dependent and didn't like it one bit.

Pouring every ounce of irritation she could muster into her glare, Ellie turned to him. "And just where the hell am I gonna go?"

He leaned over, close enough she could see the flecks of yellow gold in his eyes. Could smell the faint scent of the cinnamon candies he'd spent the last hundred miles eating. Without her consent her gaze dropped to his mouth. His tongue darted out, wetting his full bottom lip. This was bad. This was very, very bad.

"Be careful, Ellie. One day that sassy mouth of yours

might get you into trouble." His voice was low and steady. Seductive.

Her body loosened, heated, stirred between her legs.

From the first time he kissed her, Booker had been able to do that to her. Ramp her up. Play to her senses. Turn her on like no man before or after, and then make her fly.

No. There will be no ramping. No playing. No flying.

Ellie almost groaned.

God, she missed sex. She missed the intimacy of being held and touched and stroked. The feeling of warm skin pressed against her, inside her.

One side of Booker's mouth curled slowly upward.

Hers went the opposite direction.

Damn him. What kind of game was he playing? Teasing her was nothing short of cruel after he'd basically laid the entire responsibility of their failed marriage at her feet.

"Not today." She turned her burning cheeks away. She hoped he took the gesture as a dismissal and not what it really was—an attempt to hide the embarrassment of being so easily aroused.

"Don't be so sure," he growled and got out of the truck, slamming the door behind him.

Ellie groaned and covered her eyes in frustration. Though if she were being completely honest, she also did it to stop herself from staring at Booker's firm ass.

Stop it.

Clearly, the years of unintentional abstinence were messing with her head. Booker was a gorgeous man with a body built for pleasure. Of course she would respond. What woman wouldn't?

He probably had a string of women lined up, waiting for a turn with him.

The thought shouldn't bother her, but it did. A lot.

Booker climbed back into the truck and drove them around the back of the motel, parking close to the curb.

Ellie held out her hand. "May I please have the key to my room?"

He held up a single key attached to a large plastic rectangle with the number 117 emblazoned in gold on one side. "You mean *our* room?"

Oh no. She'd shared enough space with him for one day, thank you very much.

"I'm not sharing a room with you. I want my own room. I'll pay you back for the expenses. Not just for the room. For everything."

Ellie climbed from the truck. She opened the rear door on the extended cab and wrapped her fingers around the handles of the shopping bags. Booker opened the opposite door and met her gaze.

"Not gonna happen," he said. "Not on either count." He grabbed the olive-green duffel bag from the cottage and slung it over one shoulder. He tucked the laptop under his arm. "If memory serves, the last time I turned my back on you didn't turn out so well for me. I'm not looking for a repeat performance, so you'll have to forgive me if, for the time being, I don't let you out of my sight."

The man was exhausting.

"The last time didn't work out so well for me, either. I'd appreciate it if you'd stop insinuating what happened between us was easy for me. I assure you, it wasn't." *Why?* She wanted to scream at him. *Why didn't you trust me enough to talk to me? Why didn't you fight for me? For us?* "But I see some things never change. You're still making decisions that affect me without so much as a nod in my direction."

His brow arched. "You want to have a discussion about the sleeping arrangements? All right. Let's talk." Booker shut the door and came around to her side of the truck. He crossed his beefy arms, his expression firm. "Do you have a weapon?"

"N-no," she sputtered. "But—"

"Any self-defense training?"

"No. You—"

"In other words, you don't have the tools or the experience to defend yourself if a situation arose. Would you agree?"

"It not that sim—"

"It's not an essay question, Elizabeth. Yes or no."

His use of her given name was the last straw. Ellie clenched her fists. A day's worth of frustration burst from her lips, half growl, half scream. Heat bloomed in her cheeks. She was tempted to argue, but he'd left her with no defense, the arrogant bastard.

"Fine. Yes," she spat. She wanted to wipe that satisfied smirk right off his face.

"There. We agree on something." He cocked his head and studied her. "But we're not done yet, are we? You don't believe being defenseless is a good enough reason for me to be concerned, so for the sake of argument, let's say you did have your own room. Let's say whoever wants the information you may or may not have comes calling. Even if you were able to alert me to trouble, do you have any idea what kind of damage could be done before I could get to you? Because I do. Trust me, sweetheart, you were lucky yesterday."

Ellie's blood ran cold. Her bruises proved she had at least some idea, but Booker was right. It could've been so much worse. "Do you think we've been followed?"

"I think the better question is, are you willing to take the unnecessary risk? You have me. I have both the tools and the experience. I can't fucking protect you if you're not with me, and I'll be damned if I'm going to spend the night on the hard sidewalk outside your door just so you can have some space. Hence the single room."

Booker glanced at his watch. "We good here? I've got some work to do."

He went to the door and worked the key into the lock.

"You don't have to be such a jerk about it. You aren't the one having decisions made without your wants or needs being considered."

"Oh, I put your needs ahead of mine when I chose the room, Ellie. That's the only reason there are two beds instead of one."

———

BOOKER WORKED the handle harder than necessary and flung open the motel room door. The room wasn't special. It was small, but adequate for their overnight stay.

On one side of the room were the two aforementioned full-sized beds, covered with tacky bedspreads, with a night-stand set in-between. On the other side of the room, a desk with a small flat screen TV perched on one end. The door at the opposite end of the room must lead to the bathroom.

Booker led Ellie inside, motioning to the farthest bed as he secured the locks on the door. "You take that one."

He dropped his bag on the bed closest to the door, staking a claim before Ellie could argue. Not that she'd win. If trouble followed them to the motel, it would reach him first.

He placed the laptop on the desk and dug around in his bag until he found the power cord. He plugged it in and powered it up.

He could feel Ellie's eyes on him, watching him as one might a dangerous animal encountered in an unexpected place. He couldn't blame her after the bomb he'd just dropped.

All goddamned day he'd fought with the memories of how things had gone down between them. The deeper he dug, the more he didn't like what he found. Over and over he relived the scenes in his head. Every conversation they had about the military. His actions the day he joined up. He could make an argument that Ellie had known the military was what he wanted. But when it came right down to it, she hadn't known for sure what he was up to until it was too late.

He hated the idea that Ellie had been right. Not because that meant he was wrong, but because it meant he had been a total asshole to the only woman he ever loved.

If that realization hadn't been enough to darken his mood, his mental exploration of their relationship had taken a detour down naked lane.

Alone and trapped in the truck with Ellie and her tropical scent, watching her lip plump the longer she chewed on it, watching her long, jean-clad legs open and close as she shifted in her seat had been pure torture. Picturing her in those panties she'd tossed into the cart had almost been his undoing.

Fucking Christ.

He'd been hard for the better part of the day and fighting to keep his hands off her.

And now she knows it. Way to go. Way to stay focused.

Ellie shuffled behind him. "You never remarried."

"I assume you don't need confirmation since that didn't sound like a question."

"Why?"

"You know why." Did she think he'd been kidding when he stood before God and family and promised to love her until the day he died?

Men say things all the time that they don't mean.

Apparently, the joke was on him, because he kept his promises.

"I tried to get in touch with you."

He glanced over his shoulder at her. Her new flip flops had been tossed to the floor. She was sitting on the end of the bed, legs crossed.

"When? Last night?"

"About a week after the attorney sent the papers."

Shit. He turned back to the laptop. Talking about their failed marriage wasn't something he wanted to do while his dick was still hard. "The divorce papers you signed and had forwarded to the base? Those the papers you're referring to?"

"Forget it," she huffed. "I'm going to take a shower and go to bed."

Booker cursed. "No. Wait." He reached out and took her wrist as she tried to move around him, intending to apologize.

Her skin was soft and warm. Her pulse jumped under his fingertips. Booker had a stupid impulse to feel that beat against his lips and he went with it. Raised her delicate wrist to his mouth and got his first taste of her in twelve years.

She gasped on contact and his lips absorbed the jolt.

"Booker."

Oh yeah. He was a goner. "Why did you try to get in touch with me, Ellie?" he muttered, encouraged when she didn't pull away. Her pulse raced against his lips. "Tell me."

He brushed the tip of his nose along the curve of her

hand. She untucked her fingers and he moved in, pressing a light kiss to the center of her palm.

Yeah, baby. That's it. Open up for me.

"I-it's not important. It doesn't matter anymore. It won't change anything."

"Won't it?" He flicked the tip of her thumb with his tongue. "Maybe what you have to say will change everything."

"How can it?" she asked softly. "It's been too long. Too much time has passed."

He brought her hand to his heart and held her there, letting her feel the erratic beat. "Says who? Nobody here but the two of us, and I say it's never too late. It's true we can't change the past, but I think whatever it is you want to say matters a great deal, *querida*, if you're bringing it up now. Tell me."

She spoke to the floor. "I was angry. Angry and hurt and alone." She sucked in a breath and her head snapped up. Her cocoa eyes were shining with tears as her hand flew to her mouth. "Good lord. How did I not realize...? I did the exact thing I had blamed you for doing. I made a decision that affected your life without a word to you about it."

"You wanted out. What was there to discuss?"

"I didn't want out. You were my husband and I loved you. I thought you wanted out, remember? That thing you said to me about being done?"

"I already told you that's not what I meant."

"I understand that now. At the time it made sense. You joined the military the first month of our marriage. When I was excited about making a home with you and starting our lives together, you were excited about leaving me behind."

That was bullshit. Booker opened his mouth to argue,

but she held up her free hand, the one he didn't have in a death grip against his chest.

"I didn't say I was right. I was young, Booker. Hiring that attorney was stupid and impulsive and I regretted it almost immediately. That's why I tried to reach you. The man I spoke with at the base said he couldn't tell me where you were or what you were doing, but swore he'd get you the message to call me."

Booker cursed. He hadn't gotten any message. "I can't give you the details, except to tell you the op was last minute and I was gone for several months."

"You warned me that might be a possibility."

"Do you remember who you spoke with?" Booker wanted to know whose ass he was going to kick.

Ellie shook her head. "No, but I tried again after a few weeks. Same guy, same response. I had no idea if you'd gotten my package. I didn't know what to do. Then one day my attorney called and said he received the documents and that you'd signed them..." A tear slid down her cheek and she lifted one shoulder. "That was that. Eventually, I heard from Brandon. The two of you had been gone close to two years by then. The divorce had been final for a few months. He told me you had volunteered for a special task force and wouldn't be coming back to the states for a while."

"I couldn't stand the thought of being home without you. Being away made it easier."

"Why didn't you call me?" Her voice was weak and full of pain.

"Ah, hell. I don't know, Ellie. Getting those papers did something to me. In here." He squeezed her hand and tapped it against his chest. "I wanted to fight the divorce, but how was I going to do that from thousands of miles away? I had just been informed my stay overseas had been extended six months to a year. I felt helpless and out of control. I didn't understand. Like you, I was angry and hurt. I kept staring at your signature, wondering what you'd been thinking as you wrote it there. The only thing I could come up with was the obvious. You didn't want to be married to me anymore. I hated it, but my love for you wouldn't allow me to keep you if you didn't want to be kept."

Her tears were more than he could stand. He pulled her into his arms and tucked her head under his chin. "Don't do that. Don't cry, Ellie."

"I'm sorry, Booker. I never meant to hurt you."

He believed her. "I'm sorry, too, *querida*. You were the most precious thing in my life, and I'll never forgive myself for giving you reason to believe otherwise."

She sniffed and pulled back, looking up at him with those big brown eyes he could lose himself in.

"I'm glad we got that settled. I don't think I could stand another day in the truck with you being so broody."

"Broody?" Booker laughed, and the tension drained right out of him. "You think I was quiet because of the fight we left unfinished this morning?"

"Weren't you?"

"In part," he admitted and decided to hit her with another truth. "The other part of me was trying not to imagine how you would look wearing nothing except those panties I bought, as I put your sassy mouth to work on something other than taunting me."

7

E llie was not prepared for the onslaught of sensations Booker's blunt words provoked. Her abs clenched as her lungs emptied with a whoosh. Fiery sparks ignited her blood, and since her heart was racing, it didn't take long for the heat to reach every part of her body.

"I-I..." Damn it. She cleared her throat and tried again. "I thought you said we weren't safe. It might be best if we kept our clothes on. In case we have to make another run for it."

"I can be very effective, clothed or not. Or don't you remember?"

"I remember," she said on a shaky breath.

For all their history, Booker made her nervous. She'd only been with one other man, and that had been years ago. Her body had changed. She was out of practice. If the pure sexual energy pouring out of her ex-husband was any indication, he was not.

What if she disappointed him? She wouldn't be able to stand it. Plus, they were mere minutes into their new understanding. What did it all mean? What kind of relationship would they have now, if any? Were they going to be friends? One-time lovers?

"I can see you working through all the angles," he said. "And you're right. It's too soon and there are still things we need to figure out."

It was scary how well he could still read her. "Like who broke into my house, and who tried to run us down last night?"

His hold on her hip tightened. "Like why those things should be top priority in my head, but the only thing I can think about right now is tasting you." His head dipped until his breath warmed her lips. "Will you let me, Ellie? Will you let me have a taste?" His heavy-lidded gaze implored her. "Come on, sweetheart. I'm starving here."

Ellie tilted her head ever so slightly and their lips brushed. His full bottom lip was a temptation she couldn't deny. She licked at him.

Booker growled. He bent, wrapped an arm around her waist, and crushed her against his body. He fused their mouths, barely giving her time to adjust the feel of him before he pressed his tongue past her lips and into her mouth.

He explored her with honed precision, each stroke of his tongue soothing her nerves until there was no worry about the next minute, the next hour, the next week. There was only *him*.

"You feel so good," he said against her lips. He rocked his shoulders and her nipples rejoiced at the friction caused as his chest moved against hers.

She grabbed onto his neck, trying to get closer, to deepen the contact. "So good," she agreed, lost to him, to the familiar promise in his kiss. "I might've been wrong about that not getting naked thing."

She hooked her ankles around the back of his thighs and rocked against his impressive erection. "We should rethink that."

Booker's hands slid around and cupped her ass. He followed her choppy rhythm, grinding his hard length against her. His laugh was dark and dirty. "Look at you. Greedy little thing riding my dick like you can't wait another second to have it buried deep."

Ellie froze. Oh, God. What was she doing?

You climbed your ex-husband like a tree and proceeded to hump him like a bitch in heat.

Humiliated by her response to him, Ellie hid her face in the curve of his neck. "I'm sorry. I don't know what—Oh!"

She gasped as his hand came down on her ass with a quick slap. She jerked back, searching his expression for a sign of displeasure. All she found was a boatload of hot, aroused Booker.

"Don't you dare apologize," he warned. "I've been dying to get my hands on you all day. I want you greedy. I want you wet and aching and begging for my mouth, my cock. I want you any way I can have you."

She yelped when he spun around and dropped them onto the bed. He cradled her against his chest, protecting her head when they bounced.

His declarations aroused and confused her. He spent the day wanting her? She could hardly believe it. She'd been the thorn to his bear paw, just not in the way she thought.

He wanted her.

"Booker." His name was all she could manage. His heavy weight pressed her into the mattress. Muscled thighs spread hers wide to accommodate his hips.

"There will be time for all of that later. Tonight, I want to touch you. You want my hands, don't you, baby?"

She closed her eyes as he trailed soft kisses across her jaw and down her neck.

"Answer me."

"Yes," she groaned, too far gone to give him any other answer. "I want your hands. I want your mouth. I want your ... your cock."

The words felt wicked and dirty and so, so right.

Ellie felt a vibration from his chest as he buried his face against her neck. A string of Spanish flowed from his lips. He thanked God for her answer, and then proceeded to list the things he wanted to do to her in such explicit detail he surely lost any heavenly graces he might've earned with the gratitude.

She nipped his earlobe. "I understand every word you're saying, you know."

His head snapped up. A roguish gleam brightened his eyes as he rolled off her. He settled onto his side, head propped on one hand, his body stretching the length of hers and then some. "Then you won't be surprised when I do this."

He released the button on her jeans. His fingers danced along the strip of skin he bared, making her belly jump.

"Your shirt and bra," he said. His gaze darted to something behind her. The door? "Lift them, but don't take them off."

Had he heard something? Was he worried about someone trying to get in? Of course he was. The whole reason they were there was because someone had found them at the cottage.

His gaze returned to her. "We're okay for now. I'll keep you safe," he said, reading her mind again. "The only thing you need to worry about is how fast you're going to show me what I'm dying to see. Do it now, Ellie."

Her fingers shook as she followed his instructions. The moment her breasts were freed, a sudden burst of self-consciousness hit her and she covered them with her hands. Her waist hadn't been the only place that had suffered a loss of weight.

He caressed her belly, his brows pinched. "This bruise makes me mental. Are you in pain?"

Pain? What?

"No." Tender, maybe, but whatever ache she felt in her ribs had been replaced by a lower, more urgent one.

He nodded once and tugged on her wrists. "Don't hide yourself from me."

"They're not as big as they used to be." The words sounded silly once she heard them out loud, but he had loved her breasts before.

"They're perfect."

"How do you know? You haven't seen them yet."

"Show me."

Ellie closed her eyes and dropped her hands. She sucked in a breath as her nipples were simultaneously assaulted. On one side, warm and wet. On the other, the sinful pressure of being plumped.

She lifted her lids to the sight of Booker's mouth and fingers working her nipples. Her pale skin seemed to glow under his darker tone.

"*Please*," she begged, satisfying the last of his list of wants. She already checked off the greedy, wet, and aching portions of the list.

Booker took her nipple between his teeth. He nipped, soothed with his tongue, then suckled her. Nipped, soothed, suckled. Over and over. Each time harder, more insistent than the last.

A delicious pressure began to build between her legs.

She savored it, reveled in the fact she could still feel intensely sexual after such a long drought.

She wanted more.

Ellie arched her hips in a silent invitation Booker readily accepted. He abandoned her breasts. He slid his hand down her body. Tiny sparks of sensation fired everywhere he touched, leaving her skin sensitive and alive.

He dropped his mouth to her ear. "You're so soft and beautiful. I could spend hours exploring your gorgeous body. And once we put our troubles behind us, I will do just that. For now, I'll settle for making you come."

"*Yes.*" She wanted to come by a hand not her own. It had been so long.

Booker worked her zipper and slipped his hand into her panties. "*Dios mio.* You're so wet."

Ellie shook and groaned as his thick finger slid between the lips of her sex. Her hips jerked as his finger whispered over her clit, then slid down to circle her entrance. Up and back. Up and back.

Tension coiled in her belly.

Not enough.

She turned her head, searching for his face. Seeming to know what she needed, his mouth covered hers. Their tongues tangled as his fingers played with her sex.

"Slide your jeans down, baby," he muttered against her mouth. "Give me room to work."

She lifted her hips to follow his command and gasped as his finger slid inside her. "How am I supposed to do that with your hand down my pants?"

"Sorry," he murmured. "Couldn't resist." He pulled his hand away. "Go ahead."

His gaze lowered as she hooked her thumbs under the waistband of her jeans. She shoved them, along with her panties, down and worked one leg free. She rolled to face him. She threw a leg over his hip, opening herself up for whatever he wanted to do to her.

He didn't waste time. He reached between their bodies and pushed his finger back inside her. He pumped once and added another finger.

Ellie captured his mouth in a kiss so fierce it left them both panting.

Booker added a third finger and she hissed at the stretch. She rocked her hips and focused on relaxing around him.

"That's it, Ellie. Work yourself on my fingers. Christ, you're perfect. You make me forget everything except how badly I want to be inside you."

Yes, yes, yes!

"Do it. I want you there."

His thumb pressed against her clit and she shattered. Her body shook and clamped around the fingers that continued to move within her as liquid fire traveled through her veins. The room spun, but Booker's hold on her kept her from floating away.

He kissed her cheek, her nose, her eyelids. "I've never seen a more beautiful woman in my life. *Mi querida*. I've missed you."

Ellie trailed her hands down his chest. She curled her fingers around the waistband of his jeans. "We're not done."

His sigh was tortured. "We are for now. I don't have a condom. I didn't exactly plan for this to happen."

"You don't need one. I'm clean and protected. Unless..."

His jaw twitched. "I'm clean, but I'm still not going to fuck you."

She cupped his erection through his jeans and squeezed. "Are you sure about that?"

He caught her wrist. "You're not helping."

She squeezed him again, drawing a groan from his throat. "Good. I'm not trying to help unless it's to get you unzipped. Please, Booker. You need to come and I need you to be inside me when you do. *Please.*"

"Damn you." Booker tore at the fastening on his jeans. "This isn't how I wanted this to go down."

Ellie couldn't hide the smile that spread her lips.

BOOKER GLANCED AT THE DOOR.

He shouldn't be doing this. He should tuck his aching dick back into his pants and get off the bed.

There were two good reasons he didn't. The first was the confidence he had that they were safe for the night. They hadn't been followed and no one knew where they had stopped, not even Brandon.

The second reason was the wet, pink flesh waiting to be filled and the sound of his Ellie's pleas that he get on with it.

Watching her come had ranked in the top five of the greatest things he'd ever seen. He would be hard pressed to decide on the other four, but sure as shit each one involved his gorgeous wife. Yeah, *wife*. Fuck what the law said. He didn't need a piece of paper to know he would love this woman his entire life.

I didn't want out.

Ellie hadn't wanted the divorce. He hadn't wanted the divorce.

Hope blossomed within his chest, fragile and delicate and groggy from sleep.

Twelve years was a long time. They would have to get to

73

know each other again, which was a ridiculous thought when he was about to fuck the daylights out of her.

One thing at a time. There was no rush.

"Booker? Is everything okay?"

Ellie rolled onto her back. She opened her legs and dropped her knees to the sides. She teased a finger over the bare, wet lips of her pussy.

Okay, maybe there was a little rush.

"Yeah, baby. Everything's good." And because he couldn't resist, he shoved her hand out of the way. He bent and swiped the flat of his tongue through her slit.

She gasped and the upper half of her body jerked up from the bed. "*Oh my god.*"

"Sweet Jesus, you taste like the sweetest fucking candy." He took another taste. *Fuck.* So good. If he didn't stop now, he'd spend the next hour feasting between her legs.

Soon, he promised.

"Come to the edge of the bed, Ells." He shoved his jeans and underwear down to his thighs and fisted his engorged cock. "This is going to be fast and furious."

He was confident, not stupid. Until the threat was identified and eliminated there was always a risk, and he didn't want to get caught with his pants down—literally.

Her eyes widened as she watched him stroke. Her rapt attention made it impossible for him to form words so he tapped her leg to get her moving.

She scrambled to the edge of the bed, jeans and panties still hanging off one leg. His were around his thighs. Her tank top and bra were rucked up over her breasts and he still had on his T-shirt. He was a fucking animal taking her this way. She deserved so much more than a quick fuck in a motel room.

"Stop thinking so hard. I don't care about anything

except you being inside me. And maybe that you lose the shirt." Ellie bit her lip and stared at his chest. "Yeah, take that off so I can see your tattoo."

Booker reached back and pulled the shirt over his head. He tossed it onto the bed. He fell over her, catching himself with a hand on the bed in time to prevent landing on her.

Her fingers danced over the eagle on his chest. "It's gorgeous. When did you get it?"

Booker ran his fisted cock up and down her sex, coating his head with her arousal. "Six years ago."

She shuddered when he hit her clit, causing her tits to jiggle. Yeah. He wasn't going to last five seconds once he got inside her.

She traced one of the loose feathers inked on his chest. She trailed to the ones on his biceps and explored those too. "Is there a significance to the feathers?"

He licked his fingers and shoved them between her legs. Not that she needed the extra moisture. She was slick and ready for him. He lined up with her entrance, pressed in.

"One for every man lost from my battalion," he told her through his teeth. God, she was hot. And tight. Even as wet as she was, he couldn't slam home without hurting her.

Her breath hitched. "There are so many," she whispered.

"Can we talk about my tat later, Ells?" *Fuck.* "I need you to relax. I don't want to hurt you."

"You're not hurting me. You promised me fast and furious." She wrapped her legs around his ass. "Give me that."

If his woman wanted fast and furious...

Using quick, short strokes, he worked his way into her. Once she'd taken most of him, he reared back and slammed home. *Home.*

"You okay?"

"Perfect." She reached down and touched him where they were joined, making him see stars.

"Damn right, you are."

He kissed her hard and straightened. He slipped his arms under her knees and tugged her tighter against him. She was so tight, so hot around him, he nearly lost his mind.

Over and over he drove into her. His Ellie. His wife was in his arms once again, and this time, he refused to fuck it up.

She cried out a second before her body clamped around him like a vice. A garbled noise tore from his own throat as he came hard enough to blur his vision.

Sweaty and panting, Booker released her legs, chuckling when they dropped like wet noodles. Bracing himself on his hands, he leaned down and kissed her.

She smiled. "Please tell me we can do that again."

Booker laughed, his chest feeling lighter than it had in years. "Anytime you want, *querida*. Any. Time."

8

"How do you do this all day long?" Booker complained. "*Dios mio.* I'm gonna need a gallon of coffee to get through the next batch."

Ellie laughed, her fingers flying over the keyboard as Owen Jennings' voice filled the cab of the truck. She'd been working on and off for most of the day, thanks to Alec Martin's technological expertise and Noah's secure wifi device. Booker wanted to listen to the files anyway, so Ellie had decided to kill two birds with one stone. Regardless of what they found—which so far had been nothing unusual—she needed the income from transcribing the audio files.

Alec had worked his magic and downloaded the software to the laptop Booker said belonged to Noah, a former Marine who had served with him along with Roman, Sully, Ketcher, Brandon, and Adam. She couldn't remember their last names, but Booker had told her all about the guys and how Ketcher's girlfriend Regan dubbed them *the deadly seven*.

The nickname made Ellie nervous. It implied Booker had skills she couldn't conceive. That the generous, loving man she had been married to was now a deadly force to be reckoned with.

He hadn't answered her about killing the man who had hit him on the head, but Ellie suddenly had no doubt the man had died by Booker's hands. The same hands that had given her pleasure last night.

The dichotomy between the two sides of him was staggering and she was struggling to wrap her head around it.

"What's the deal with this guy, anyway?" Booker asked.

Ellie stopped the recording. She'd missed the last couple of minutes anyway and would have to go over it again. "What do you mean?"

"When did you start working for him?"

"Ten years ago."

"Have you always worked from home?"

"No. I was Owen's administrative assistant for the first two years."

"What happened during year three?"

Ellie automatically reached for the locket around her neck. She thumbed the warm metal.

"My mom got sick. ALS." Amyotrophic lateral sclerosis, a rare neurodegenerative disease with no cure.

The initial prognosis hadn't been good. Five years, max, they'd said. Her mom had survived for eight.

When it became obvious her mom would need a full-time caregiver, Ellie gave up her apartment and moved back home. By then her mom had bought a modest house in a quiet Austin suburb. Ellie still lived there, but the house had become part of her mother's estate after she died. Her mom didn't have insurance of any kind and medical expenses had driven up the debt. At this point, Ellie wasn't sure if she would get to keep the house. "She died six months ago."

"Oh, baby," Booker took her hand and raised it to his

lips. The gentle kiss he placed on her knuckles melted her heart. "I'm so sorry."

"Thank you." Ellie hadn't spoken to anyone about the years of taking care of her mother. Before she knew it, words were flowing out of her mouth.

"You knew my mom. She provided enough to keep the authorities from taking me away, but she wasn't big on affection and time. We were never close and her illness made her bitter. The first few years were the worst. She hated everything and everyone. She complained about the doctors and nurses. I couldn't do anything right. She threw things. She lashed out and yelled constantly."

Ellie hated herself for it, but it was almost a relief when her mom deteriorated to the point she couldn't use her arms or voice box anymore.

"Why didn't you put her in a facility tailored to the kind of care she needed?"

"She was all I had. I might not have had a perfect childhood, but it could've been worse. I couldn't turn my back on her. She provided for me when she didn't have to."

"The fuck she didn't. Ells. She was your *parent*. That's the very definition of *have to*."

"I agree with you, but my father didn't see it that way. He took off and never looked back. My mom could've done that, too, but she didn't. And it wasn't all bad. She made an effort to be there for me after you and I got married. She helped me decorate the house after you deployed. It wasn't much, and she never stayed for more than an hour or two, but it was more than she'd done in the past."

Ellie swallowed hard, hoping she hadn't disrupted the peaceful ease between them by bringing up the past.

Booker squeezed her hand reassuringly. "I'm glad she was there for you, if only to rearrange furniture. A lot of the guys used to talk about how hard deployment was on the wives and families. I should've made sure my parents were there for you."

"If I remember correctly, they had their hands full with Annabel." Booker's younger sister had been a terror after he joined the military.

"Anna's poorly timed rebellion was no excuse. I should've paid more attention. Been more sensitive to what you were going through. I am sorry, Ells."

"Thank you, but you don't need to keep apologizing. I forgave you last night."

He shot her a wink. "And again in the shower this morning."

Her thighs clenched at the reminder and she shot him a look. Had it only been a day and a half since he'd come back into her life? It felt as though they'd never been apart.

"Annnyway," she said. "We were talking about Owen and why I started working from home. Mom had no income, so I had to keep my job. I explained the situation and Owen was happy to accommodate. I took over all of the transcription duties for the office, since that was the only task the firm needed that I could do remotely. It wasn't easy, but eventually I adjusted to living on little sleep."

Even now she had trouble sleeping for more than a couple of hours at a time.

"Owen was very patient during those first months while I found my way. He's been good to me, all things considered."

"All what things considered?"

Ellie shrugged, not sure where to begin. She had struggled to transition into a world where there was no one to care for but herself. For a few weeks, she hadn't tried. She stuck to the same routine, using the time she would've spent caring for her mom to rid the house of her mom's illness. She returned medical equipment and tossed leftover supplies. She cleaned. Rearranged rooms. All the while dealing with the legalities that came with the loss of a loved one.

Legalities Owen had offered to help her through. Owen had been more than her boss. He encouraged her to get out of the house. He took her out for coffee. He'd been a friend. A confidante.

Until everything changed.

"After Mom died, I didn't know what to do. There were so many debts. Owen offered to handle all of the legal aspects of Mom's estate, and I said yes. I knew Owen felt more for me than I did for him, but it was innocent, you know?"

"How innocent?"

"For years, he didn't proposition me or do anything to make me uncomfortable. He was ... friendly. He checked up on me. He tried to help with Mom, but that's where I drew the line. He was my boss, but I'd be lying if I said it wasn't nice to have someone who cared."

Booker kept his gaze on the highway. A muscle in his cheek twitched. "And then what happened?"

"About a month after Mom died, Owen changed. He became more demanding, more possessive. He wanted to know where I was and who I was with. He started making declarations and referring to our lives together. I humored him to a point, because I need my job, but I immediately began searching for new employment."

"Humored him how?"

Booker's calm, quiet tone made her shiver. Instinct told her to tread lightly.

"I went to dinner with him on occasion. I answered his

questions about my schedule, because I didn't see the point in not. I didn't balk if he put his hand on my lower back and guided me through a restaurant. But that's as far as it went. Whenever he tried to kiss me or pull me into a hug, I resisted. In the last few weeks, his insistence has grown to an uncomfortable level."

"You think he will stop taking no for an answer."

It wasn't a question, but Ellie answered anyway. "That's my fear, yes. He's arrogant. I have no doubt he believes he will have me whether I want him or not."

"You think he would rape you? A man with lofty political aspirations?"

"He's also a highly intelligent, well-respected attorney with a list of powerful clients. I'm just a typist. Do you think anyone would take my word over his?" Ellie shoved her fingers through her hair. "I want to believe he wouldn't hurt me, but I just don't know."

"He's not going to hurt you, Ells. I promise you that. And no matter what we find on those flash drives, you might as well go on and give notice. You're done working for that prick."

She sighed. "It's not that simple."

"The hell it isn't."

Ellie turned in her seat to face him. "I'm going to quit—"

"Good."

"—But not before I find another job."

"Ellie—"

She put a hand up, cutting him off. It had been bothering her since last night and she had to get this off her chest.

"I don't know what's going on between us, but at some point soon I'll have to go back to Austin. I have responsibilities and I need to work. And there's my mom's estate to consider. Like it or not, Owen is the gatekeeper of information until I can make other arrangements. If I end up losing the house, I'll have to pack everything and figure out where I'm going to live."

The details were overwhelming. She took a deep breath. "I will quit. I will. But like I said, it's complicated."

"So un-complicate it."

She snorted. "I wish I could."

"You can," Booker insisted.

"Oh, really? How do you suggest I do that?"

"You can quit your fucking job and stay in Montana with me."

9

"And this is the kitchen." Booker flipped on the portable work lights and held back the plastic barrier that separated the kitchen from the living area. "Watch your step."

He'd been saying that a lot as he guided Ellie through a tour of the main house. Booker was happy to see his foreman, Mike Fitzpatrick, had kept things moving during his absence, but the place was still a construction zone. There wasn't one completed room in the whole house. Everywhere he looked there were power tools, sawhorses, paint buckets, brown paper, and plastic sheeting.

"Oh, Booker," Ellie breathed as she stepped into the room.

"What do you think?"

Ellie had been quiet since he suggested she stay in Montana with him. She hadn't given him an answer. He knew it was too soon, but damn it, they'd lost enough time. The way she'd come apart in his arms last night was proof she still felt something for him. He wanted to explore that and see where it would take them.

Learning she hadn't wanted the divorce had done something to him. It was as if that one detail had loosened the invisible grip that had stifled the effectiveness of his heart and lungs for so long.

He could fucking *breathe* again and he wanted another chance to do right by her. To be the man she needed.

He wouldn't even pressure her to live with him in the cabin, although it would kill him not to have her in his bed every night.

She could live in the house with his family while they got reacquainted. He would give her whatever she wanted as long as she stuck around and gave them a fair chance.

As Ellie turned in a circle to take in the huge space, Booker kneeled to inspect a box of imported Spanish tile. The tile wasn't to his taste, but this space wasn't for him. *Abuelita* would love the colorful backsplash and the reminder of home, so it was worth every penny.

"It's wonderful. I can almost smell the delicious meals that will be cooked here."

He brushed off his hands and straightened. He glanced around, trying to see past the dust and disarray to see what Ellie saw.

The rust colored floor tiles had been laid. The large center island was in place and had plenty of seating for casual meals. The bright white cabinets were hung and the stainless-steel appliances were installed. He particularly liked the recessed lighting and exposed ceiling beams.

All in all, the kitchen would be worthy of its place as the heart of the house.

"Speaking of which, are you hungry? I can't promise to cook anything near as delicious as *Abuelita's* paella, but I can make a mean grilled cheese with mustard and potato chips sandwich."

Ellie's delighted laugh warmed his chest. "I haven't had one of those in ages."

"They used to be your favorite." God, he was a fucking sap for this woman. He extended a hand to her. "Shall we go?"

She nodded and took one last look around before taking his hand.

"It's so peaceful here," she said as they strolled the seventy-five yards to his cabin to the sounds of crickets chirping.

"Wait'll you get a load of the foothills at sunrise."

"I can't wait. Do I hear water?"

"You do. There's a stream that runs through the property." Booker pointed in the general direction. "Over that way."

"I can see why you picked this place." Her sigh was full of longing.

Good. He wanted her to love it so much she wouldn't want to leave.

"The place kind of picked me, actually."

"How so?"

He shrugged. "I got out of the military without a plan for what I might do for work."

"Couldn't you have gone to work with Brandon?"

Brandon and his siblings owned a specialized training center outside of Austin. Brandon had made him an offer, but Booker turned him down. Austin was the last place he wanted to live. If the memories weren't enough, the idea that he could run into Ellie with another man cinched the relocation deal.

"I spent enough time with that joker on the battlefield. You think I wanted to keep seeing his ugly mug every day?"

She rolled her eyes. "Ha. Ha. All right, funny guy. Finish your story."

He relaxed into the explanation. "A mutual Marine buddy gave James my number and he contacted me. He was looking for retired military professionals for his relatively new business, Kent Protection Service. We spoke on the phone and it sounded like a good fit. As it turns out, I was right. So, I hired a real estate agent. She wasn't optimistic about finding what I was looking for in the price range I needed." He spread his arms wide. "But this place went on the market the very next day. The sellers were overseas and wanted to unload the property fast. It was the perfect place. A house for my family. A cabin for me. I made an offer that day."

"I think it's nice that you're moving your family up here to be with you. A lot of guys wouldn't do something like that."

"I think we've already established I'm not like the men who say things they don't mean and shirk their responsibility to family."

A gorgeous blush creeped into her cheeks. "Fair enough. What do you do for James?"

"Personal security."

"You're a bodyguard? Do you have to travel a lot?"

"I am, but last week was the first time I've left Montana in a year, and it had nothing to do with my job." He sighed, knowing he had to be real with her. "But there is always the possibility I will have to travel with a client. Does the thought of me being gone on assignment bother you?"

She seemed to consider his question. "Other than the obvious reasons, I don't see why it would."

"What obvious reasons?"

She stopped walking and turned to face him. She put her hands on his shoulders and went up on her toes. Booker leaned down and met her half way, but she stopped short of their lips touching.

"Not being able to do this every day," she purred.

Holy shit. Her mouth was the sweetest honey he ever tasted. As she melted against him, Booker made a mental note to inform James he wouldn't be accepting any out of town jobs.

He ended the kiss before he lost control and fucked her right there in the yard. His heart pounded against his ribcage. "Does that mean you'll stay?"

"We still have a lot to figure out, and there are things I need to do in Austin, but yes. I'd like to spend some time with you."

Booker crowded her personal space. He slipped his hand around the back of her neck and kissed her, hard and deep. "To be continued after we eat and check in with Brandon," he growled against her lips.

"Promise?"

"You're damn right I do. I hope you're not too tired. I plan to keep you up all night."

The smile she gave was sexy and full of sass. "Funny, I thought that was my line."

God, he fucking loved her.

"What did I tell you about that mouth?" He popped her ass, making her jump with a squealed laugh.

When they reached the cabin, he climbed the wide steps and went to the front door. He stomped his boots against the mat, then opened the door and stood back, allowing Ellie room to go ahead of him.

The cabin was nothing more than a gigantic square with a porch all the way around. It had been built for efficiency with little wasted space. One bedroom, one bath. A decent sized living room and a small kitchenette. Nothing fancy. It had suited his needs, but his needs were changing by the minute.

Booker handed Ellie his cell phone. "Do you want to get Brandon on the line while I whip us up some sandwiches?"

He grabbed a frying pan and supplies from the refrigerator. He opened the cupboard and pulled down a bag of potato chips.

"Hey, Bran," Ellie said into the phone. "Good. Uh, huh. Booker's place. Couple of hours ago. Yeah. It's amazing."

She winked at him as he lined up six pieces of bread along the counter. Everything about the scene felt right. Ellie in his home. Talking to their shared, life-long friend on the phone. Even the crazy-ass grilled cheese he was about to make for her.

Ellie joined him by the stove. "I'm going to put you on speaker. Okay, Booker can hear you now."

She held the phone between them.

"Hey, Spaniard." Brandon's voice vibrated through the line.

"What up, Blondie? You looking out for my girls?"

"You sound ... chipper. It's kinda freaking me out. Where's the gruff and tough asshole I know and love?"

"Aw, you love me? That's so fucking sweet, 'mano."

"Don't get excited. You're not my ty—"

"Guys!" Ellie interrupted, her tone a mixture of humor and exasperation.

And because he could, Booker leaned over and pecked her lips. He had twelve years of kisses to make up for. He planned to take advantage of every opportunity.

"All right, all right. Yeah, Book, your girls are good. I spent the evening moving packed boxes to the garage, when I wasn't on the phone with Alec, that is."

"I appreciate you being there to help and keep an eye. What's the news?"

He traced the line of Ellie's jaw with his fingers. She was so beautiful. He would never get tired of looking at her. Touching her. His mouth watered for another taste, but he settled for another quick kiss before he returned to the sandwiches.

"Not much, I'm afraid. I've reached out to some of our contacts, but there's no chatter to link the SUV to the situation with Ketcher. From what I've been able to ascertain, the crew in Florida went dark after what happened to Regan. My guess? They went underground to reorganize. They weren't responsible."

"Then what the fuck?" Booker buttered a piece of bread and tossed it into the pan. He squeezed a healthy amount of mustard on the bread, then followed it up with cheese. He tossed a few chips on top of the cheese before adding another piece of buttered bread. "You're telling me the SUV is connected to Ellie? That they did use the flash drives to track us to the cottage?"

God, he was glad he'd gotten rid of the devices. There hadn't been time nor an urgent need to secure his property. If someone wanted to get to them, Booker would have no warning save the basic alarm system installed in the cabin.

Leaning against the counter, Ellie played with her necklace, eyes glued to the sandwich he moved around in the pan. She did that a lot, he realized. Whenever she was nervous or trying to work something out in her head, she toyed with the locket.

He didn't want her worried. He wanted her safe. He would make the necessary calls tomorrow to put the appropriate security in place.

"It appears that way. Roman and Adam went out there,

but the SUV was gone by the time they arrived. The side door had been kicked in. The bedroom Ketcher had been using had been tossed. They found Ellie's bag and her stuff had been scattered around the other bedroom. The guys retrieved the drives from where you buried them. If they are somehow being tracked, those assholes will have a rude awakening when they come calling."

An awakening of the deadly seven—or six since he wasn't there—kind. Booker almost hated to miss it. He wouldn't mind expending a little energy on the fuckers who tried to hurt Ellie.

"*Oorah.*"

"*Oorah*," Brandon returned. "Alec cleaned them up and was able to pull the data. He found an encrypted folder."

Ellie pushed away from the counter. She went straight to the table and opened the laptop. "What's the folder name?"

Brandon read off a series of numbers.

Booker flipped Ellie's sandwich onto a plate and set the pan aside. He carried it to the table and set it down in front of her. "Eat."

"I don't see that folder," she said.

"Because it's hidden."

"Was Alec able to see what was in it?" Booker asked.

"He was, but we haven't been able to make any sense of it yet. There are a lot of spreadsheets to go through. Each one lists the name of a restaurant or bar—some currently in business and some not—and then a series of numbers. It appears to be an accounting of some kind, but there's no data to indicate what the numbers mean."

Booker slid into the chair next to Ellie's. "Can you give us some of the names?"

Brandon started rattling them off. When he got to the fourth name, Ellie piped up.

"I know those places. Owen set them up." Ellie shook her head. "I mean he handled all of the initial paperwork. Incorporation paperwork, employee agreements, non-disclosure agreements, that kind of thing."

"Ellie," Brandon said after a minute. "Have you ever heard the name Dean Sanchez?"

Her face scrunched in confusion. "No, why?"

"Just a hunch. I need to do some more digging. I'll get back to you as soon as something makes sense. In the meantime, stay safe."

More than once, his life had been in Brandon's hands, and vice versa. Trust was the only reason Booker didn't push.

"Always, *'mano*. Call the minute you've got something, no matter the time."

"Copy that."

Ellie shook her head as Booker ended the call. "Who do you think Dean Sanchez is?"

From the sound of it, no one Booker wanted Ellie involved with. "I don't know, but I don't want you to worry about anything. Whatever is going on, we will deal with it. I'll keep you safe."

"I'm not worried." Her expression was almost shy when she added, "I've always felt safe with you."

Her belief in him swelled his chest. He leaned over and kissed her forehead. "Thank you, *querida*. Now, go on and eat your sandwich. I've got a promise to keep."

———

"YOU'VE REACHED the voicemail of Ellie King. Please leave your name and number—"

Owen Jennings disconnected the call and slammed his fist against his polished wood desk.

How many times had he told her to change her voice-mail? Ellie was child's name. Not appropriate for the woman who would be at his side. Her given name was Elizabeth and she would damn well use it.

Owen picked up a glass of scotch and downed the contents. He poured another two fingers.

His patience was wearing thin.

Judith had one fucking task. Send Elizabeth the files for transcription. Oh, she had sent the files, all right. But she also sent the drive—the one hidden in the compartment under his phone—that could land him an all-expense-paid trip to the bottom of Lake Austin, compliments of cement boots.

Stupid, clumsy cunt. She was too homely to wear spiked heels anyway, and she obviously lacked the grace to walk properly in them. Firing Judith had been one of his greatest pleasures of the week. He didn't need her. He had Elizabeth, who would return the flash drive and resume her duties in the office and in his life.

Owen took a drink of the fresh scotch, savoring the dark, spicy flavor.

Elizabeth wasn't smart enough to figure out the significance of what she had. On the surface, the contents of the drive would appear to be nothing more than dictation files. The perfect decoy in the event the drive fell into the wrong hands.

Elizabeth's hands were far from wrong, but he'd breathe easier once she and the drive had been recovered.

He dialed his phone.

"You've reached the—"

He hung up.

"Son of a bitch." He tossed the phone on the desk. Why the hell wasn't she answering? Or calling him back?

They would definitely have a conversation about inconsiderate behavior and his expectations for future communication.

It had been over 48 hours since he'd sent Leo to find the drive while Elizabeth had been out of the house. This was all Leo's fault. The fuckwit wasn't supposed to touch her.

Owen drained the glass and poured another.

He was surrounded by idiots.

Never send a boy to do a man's job.

His father had been right. He should've handled the situation himself.

Owen stretched his hand and flexed his swollen, bruised knuckles. Leo wouldn't forget his displeasure any time soon. No one touched what belonged to him.

An alert sounded on his cell and Owen picked it up. He opened the app and relief washed over him.

Finally.

He caressed his thumb over the blinking green light.

"There you are."

He reached into his desk and pulled out a small bottle. He dabbed the thick, flesh colored liquid onto his skin until the bruises were nothing but a memory.

It wouldn't do for a future senator to travel with battered knuckles. He had an image to protect.

10

Booker swung the ax over his head. Working his muscles with practiced precision, he brought the blade down. A satisfying *crack* rent the air as the log broke apart, the halves toppling to the ground. He stacked the two pieces along with the others. He bent, grabbed another section of the large oak, and placed it on the stump.

Swing. *Crack*. Stack.

Swing. *Crack*. Stack.

He breathed in the warm mountain air and sank into the movement of the ax. He had a chainsaw in the barn, but the manual labor gave his muscles a much-needed workout. And it gave him time to think.

Brandon hadn't called.

Waiting was a necessary evil in Booker's line of work—hell, in *life*—but he fucking hated it. Some guys got off on the adrenaline build up of being leashed in limbo. He'd seen it over and over again in Afghanistan. Like dogs at the starting gate right before the doors were opened, soldiers would hunker down, get more and more pumped as they waited for the signal to move. To them, waiting was foreplay. The signal to move out was their orgasm, their high.

Not for him. Limbo gave him fucking hives. It filled him with a nervous energy so far from pleasurable he might as well be suffocating.

Hence the two hours he'd spent repairing the stalls in the barn and the current wood chopping.

Swing. *Crack*. Stack.

He paused long enough to pick up his cell phone and glare at the screen. He checked the signal. He willed the fucking thing to ring.

"What is it about a sweaty man with an ax that's so incredibly hot?"

Booker slid the phone into his back pocket. He glanced over his shoulder to find Ellie staring back at him. She looked good enough to eat in her usual jeans and tank top— a black one today.

"I can honestly say I have no idea." He swung the ax one final time, lodging it into the stump. He grabbed his T-shirt from the wood pile where he'd discarded it earlier. He swiped it over his face and down his torso.

She held out a bottle of water. "As much as I hate to interrupt such an incredible display of manliness, you looked like you could use this."

"Watching me chop wood is a turn-on?" The oak he'd been working on had died. He hadn't planned to cut down any others, but ... huh. "Good to know."

He took the bottle from her. He bent and placed a kiss on the side of her neck. "Thanks, baby."

She watched him drink, her gaze alight with mischief. "Have you worked up an appetite?"

His dick stirred. "That depends. What's on the menu?"

She spun away as he tried to pull her into his arms. He stalked toward her.

"Oh no, you don't." She held her palms out, backing away with each step he took. "While your sweaty muscles are easy to look at, I don't have a large collection of clothes to choose from. I'd like to keep these clean, if you don't mind."

He'd take care of her clothes situation tomorrow. He'd take her shopping in Bozeman and buy her whatever she needed. "You're right," he said solemnly. "Except for one thing."

"What's that?"

"I do mind."

He lunged at her. Ellie yelped, turned, and ran toward the main house.

Booker easily overtook her within a few yards. She screamed in delight as he hooked an arm around her waist and lifted her off the ground. "Where do you think you're going?"

He set her down in front of a wide oak and spun her to face him. Her cheeks were flushed, her gaze full of promise and hope and ... his heart kicked ... *love*.

She hadn't said the words, but it was right there, shining in her eyes the exact same way it had on their wedding day.

His knees almost gave out. He went at her mouth like a man possessed. And he was. With a twelve year old pent-up need for her.

He slipped a hand under her tank and palmed her breast. Her nipple beaded against the thin lace of her bra. He latched on, rolled the bud between his thumb and fore-finger. He shoved his other hand between her legs and pressed the seam of her jeans against her sex.

Damn, the heat. She was burning for him.

She rocked against his hand, moaning.

His cell phone rang. Brandon's ringtone.

No. No, no, no.

The bastard.

Booker broke the kiss and slowly removed the hand from between her legs. Panting, Booker rested his forehead against hers. Under different circumstances he might let the call of to voicemail. Not today, though.

He plumped her nipple one more time before he let her go.

"Your timing sucks, man," he said into the phone.

"I've got news."

"Tell me."

"My hunch panned out," Brandon said. "I went over the names on the spreadsheets with a friend of the family. Cooper Jackson. He's the sheriff over in Burnet County."

"And?"

"The businesses coincide with an ongoing investigation into organized crime throughout Texas."

"Mother*fuck*. Are you kidding me?"

"What is it?" Ellie asked.

Booker zeroed in on where her fingers toyed with the locket around her neck. Needing to ease her, he motioned her closer. He wrapped his arm around her and pulled her tightly to his side. He activated the speaker so they both could hear.

"I wish I were kidding," Brandon told them. "The guy I mentioned last night, Dean Sanchez? He's been on law enforcement's radar for some time under suspicion of money laundering and drug trafficking through several of his businesses."

"Let me guess, the same businesses listed in the files on Owen's flash drive?"

"You got it. Alec figured out the key to deciphering the information. Once he did that, a picture started to form."

"How is Owen involved?" Ellie asked, clearly shaken to learn her boss wasn't just a possessive douche, but a potential criminal as well.

"Owen kept a detailed account of the money moved through each company. That in itself indicates he's involved in the process on some level. Or Owen's trying to set Sanchez up for a fall, and he has someone on the inside helping him. That's for the feds to figure out. Dean Sanchez is not a good dude. Can you imagine what Dean would do to Owen if he found out the guy was keeping detailed records of his criminal dealings? We're talking Soprano's-blown-kneecaps-dirt-nap kind of shit. Not even prison would stop Sanchez from taking Owen out."

Booker swore a blue streak. "In other words, Owen will do whatever it takes to get the drive back, and he thinks Ellie has is."

Beside him, Ellie trembled. He rubbed her arm, not liking the clamminess of her skin. "It's okay, baby," he said against her ear. "We're going to get through this."

Raising his voice for Brandon to hear, he asked, "Has law enforcement picked either of them up for questioning yet?"

"You know things don't work that quickly. There's a process. It'll be soon, though. The cops have had eyes on Sanchez for the last hour or so, and as soon as they locate Owen, they'll watch him as well."

"What do you mean locate Owen?"

"He isn't at his house or at work. Don't worry. He'll turn up."

Booker tried not to tense, but panic hit him like a blow-torch to the chest. "You need to find him, Brandon. You need to find him right godda—"

A shot rang out a second before white-hot pain seared through his left side.

The phone flew from his hand. Booker was aware of Ellie reaching for him, screaming his name as he stumbled. His foot caught on a tree limb and he went down. Hard. An explosion went off in his head and his vision blurred.

"Booker!"

He tried to move, but his body wouldn't cooperate.

"Run, Ellie," he choked out. "Get out of here." *Fuck.* The pain was excruciating. "Keys...in...the truck. *Go!*"

Booker fought against the darkness that was coming for him at top speed. And lost.

THERE WAS SO MUCH BLOOD.

Ellie dropped to her knees and crawled toward Booker. "No, no. Please God, no. Booker!" Sobbing, she shook him, praying for a response. When none came, she dropped her forehead to his chest. "Please, Booker. Don't leave me. Please," she choked. "Not again."

"Get away from him, Elizabeth."

Ellie gasped as Owen Jennings stepped out from behind a tree, gun in his hand raised and ready for business.

Ellie surged to her feet. "Owen? You did this?" Her voice rose to near hysteria. Booker was bloody, possibly dead, and it was all her fault. "H-how did you find me?"

Owen's gaze dropped to her neck. "With a little help from your mother."

Her hand flew to her throat as realization dawned. "What did you do?" She ripped the locket from her neck as though it were on fire and tossed it to the ground. Too little, too late.

"When I was taking inventory of your mother's things, I found the locket. I knew you would appreciate the trinket, so I had it cleaned. I also had a minuscule tracking device embedded behind your mother's photograph." His voice rose with every word. "You weren't being cooperative. *Someone* needed to keep an eye on you. You didn't have anyone else. *I* took care of you. *I* looked out for you. *I* wanted you, and this," Owen jabbed the gun in Booker's direction. "*This is how you repay me?*"

She glanced down at Booker and her breath caught. The rise and fall of his chest was shallow, barely discernable, but it was there. Her knees threatened to buckle. He was alive.

"I *saw* you, Elizabeth," Owen spat. "You let him touch you. You let him grab your cunt and paw you like an animal. Against a tree, no less. I should've known all those times you told me 'no' you were just playing coy. You were hoping I would take what I wanted anyway. You should've told me, darling, instead of allowing this piece of shit to touch what *belongs to me*."

Owen stepped forward, a murderous glint in his eye. He would kill Booker if she didn't do something. She had to distract him, keep his focus on her.

"He's dead!" she screamed. "It doesn't matter anymore because you killed him!"

Owen's gaze darted to Booker, his expression smug.

No, no, no. Don't look at him. Look at me.

She backed away from Booker, every step like a knife in her heart.

Owen stood between her and the cabin, so there was no chance of getting to the weapon Booker had there. Booker said the keys were in the truck. She didn't want to leave him, but what other option did she have? If she could make it to the truck, she could run Owen's ass over to ensure he wouldn't finish the job he'd started.

Tears streamed her cheeks and she prayed she was making the right decision.

"And you're delusional if you believe I ever wanted *you*."

Ellie turned and ran, wagering her life and Booker's that Owen wouldn't be able to resist the chase. That his arrogance would demand he take her down and force her to submit.

She hadn't underestimated Owen's actions, but she had miscalculated his ability for speed.

Terror froze her blood when she heard the pounding of Owen's feet behind her. He'd closed the distance quicker than she expected. She'd never make it to the truck before he caught up with her.

Dodging left, she ran up the stairs leading to the back door of the main house. Lungs burning, heart pounding, she threw open the door. She darted through the living room and hit the stairs to the upper level, taking them two at a time.

As she reached the upper landing, heavy footfalls sounded below her.

She ducked into the first room she came to, but it was empty, devoid of anything she could use as a weapon.

Shit.

Her heart raced as she jogged across the hall to another room. Jackpot. Someone had left behind a tool belt. She swung the door shut as Owen reached the top of the stairs and saw her. Not finding a lock, Ellie braced her back against the door. She dug in her heels, but her weight was no match for Owen's.

He rammed the door.

The force threw her off balance, propelled her into the room as Owen stalked through the doorway.

"Don't make this harder on yourself than it needs to be, Elizabeth. We can work this out. I can forgive your indiscretion. I will have to punish you, of course, to ensure this type of thing doesn't happen again. You will learn your place and everything will be all right." He reached out for her. "Come now, darling. I just need you to give me the flash drives Judith sent to you and we can go home."

Ellie shook her head and took a step back. She faked a stumble, swiping a screwdriver from an abandoned tool belt and holding it flat against the inside of her arm. If she caught him by surprise, she might be able to incapacitate him long enough to get the gun out of his hand.

She didn't believe for one minute that Owen had any intention of letting her live. He shot Booker. Ellie could ruin him, and they both knew it.

Owen didn't realize the job had already been done for her.

"It's too late, Owen. I know the extra drive was sent to me by mistake. I know what's on it."

"Oh, Elizabeth." Owen tsked. "You don't know anything."

"I know about Dean Sanchez." Ellie prayed she hadn't just signed her own death warrant. "I know you've compiled eviden—"

Owen's expression turned thunderous and he went for her throat. He shoved her against the wall hard enough to force her lungs to empty through her constricted windpipe.

"How do you know that name?" he yelled, his fingers digging into the skin under her jaw. "You couldn't have worked through the security on those files on your own. Who helped you?" He released her throat and raised his hand. Fire exploded across her face as his palm connected with her left cheek. "Who else knows?"

Ellie struggled to breathe. Owen lifted the gun, placing the business end under her chin. A sob escaped her lips when the hand that slapped her dropped to her breast, the intimate touch making her skin crawl. He pressed the gun against her chin, forcing her head back. His eyes were cold and hard.

"It seems I underestimated you, Elizabeth. I didn't realize you had people in your life who were smart enough to decrypt files, let alone make sense of them. You led me to believe you were alone in the world once your mother died. No friends. No family. But you're not the poor little abandoned soul you claimed to be, are you?"

No. She wasn't. She had people who loved her. People she loved. She'd lost sight of that for awhile, too caught up in her own idea of what it meant to be a family. If she got out of this alive, she'd never make that mistake again.

"You're nothing but a lying whore." Stinging pain shot through her as Owen squeezed her breast. "Tell me who helped you."

From out of nowhere, anger sparked a fire in her gut, muting the gnawing fear. She would never give him the names he wanted. *Never.* She would protect the people she loved, or she would die trying.

The strength of her resolve gave her purpose and she realized this must be what Booker felt all the time. Strong in conviction. Confident in action. The power of it made her head spin.

"Go to hell."

"I will pull this fucking trigger, Elizabeth." Fast as lightning, Owen fired a shot into the ceiling and returned the gun to press against her jaw. "Tell me what I want to know or the next one ruins that pretty face of yours."

The metal burned against her skin. She was out of time.

Ellie changed the angle of the hold she had on the screwdriver and tightened her grip. She looked him dead in the eye as she lifted her arm out and used every bit of strength she had to plunge the tool into his side.

Bile rose in her throat as the screwdriver penetrated Owen's flesh. Something warm and sticky covered her shaking fingers. She looked down and immediately gagged. Blood.

Her fingers jerked loose from the screwdriver of their own accord as she sank against the wall. Owen fell back a step, his mouth open in a silent cry of surprise.

Oh, God.

She'd done it. She'd just stabbed a man. The shock of it cost her precious seconds. The next thing Ellie knew, she was staring down the barrel of Owen's gun.

11

Someone called his name.

Booker groaned and cracked his lids. Holy Christ, his head hurt. His left side was no picnic either, so he rolled right and pushed himself up. Pain sliced through his skull and he pressed the heels of his palms against his eyes in a pitiful attempt to keep his jumbled brains from seeping out.

"Goddamn it, Spaniard! Pick up the fucking phone!"

Booker turned toward the voice. Everything came back to him in a rush.

Kissing Ellie. Talking to Brandon on the phone. *The phone.*

Booker found it on the ground beside him and he put the thing to his ear. "Bran," he croaked, shoving to his feet. A muffled *thank fuck* drifted through the line. "Owen was here. Ellie—" Booker searched for any sign of her. "How long was I out?"

His head felt as if it had been split open. He felt around and sure enough, he found a gash the size of the Grand Canyon on the back of his head, compliments of the bloody rock jutting out of the ground.

"A couple of minutes. I heard the shot. Are you hit?"

Booker glanced at the wound in his left shoulder. No exit wound and still bleeding. "I'll live."

"I called James after I heard the shot. He's on the way. ETA: twenty minutes."

Booker didn't have twenty minutes. "I've got to find Ellie."

"Owen tracked her with the locket. I heard part of an argument before everything went quiet."

He needed a weapon.

As he took the first step toward the cottage, Ellie's scream broke the silence.

He spun toward the sound, dizziness making him stagger sideways like a drunk.

The house. She was in the house.

Growling with fury, Booker knew he didn't have time to get to his gun. He charged ahead, ready to take on Owen unarmed, before he remembered the ax. Willing his legs to cooperate, he doubled back, closed the short distance to the woodpile. Using his good arm, he jerked the handle of the ax, freeing it from the stump.

I'm coming, baby. Hang on.

Wanting to conserve energy, he didn't bother lifting the blade. He let it drag the ground as he forced his legs into a sloppy jog.

The uselessness of his left arm reminded him that Owen had a gun. Booker slipped through the back door without a sound.

A shot rattled the walls.

Fear and adrenaline flooded Booker's system, giving him a brief reprieve from the pain. Moving fast and quiet he made his way through the house and up the stairs.

Heart hammering in his chest, he followed the sounds.

He flattened against the wall outside the room, drew in a breath, and slipped through the doorway.

Blind rage assaulted him when he saw Owen holding a gun to Ellie's head. Her face was tear-stained and bruised.

Her eyes widened when she saw him. The fear and regret in her eyes was his undoing.

She was not dying today.

Booker swung the ax. His strength and aim were off, but the blade found purchase in the arm holding the gun.

Owen roared in agony. The gun dropped to the floor. He clawed at the blade, knocked it loose.

Before Owen could recover, Booker dove for the gun. Training and instinct took over. He palmed the grip, rolled to his back, and fired a bullet directly into Owen's skull.

The force from the shot threw Owen back and he fell to the floor, dead.

Booker stretched his neck, searching for Ellie. She was slumped on the floor. Her arms were wrapped around her knees and she was rocking slightly.

Fuck. He never wanted her to see this side of him. His life hadn't been all sunshine and roses. There were dark, ugly areas he had hoped to shield her from. He didn't want her to be afraid of him, or afraid of what she'd seen.

He rolled to his knees and hobbled over to her. His strength was running out. He'd lost a lot of blood and the bullet in his shoulder would need to be removed ASAP. Might need a few stitches in his noggin, too.

"Ellie? Baby, are you okay?"

She jumped, as if his voice startled her. He reached for her, needed to hold her, to feel her warmth and the beat of her heart.

"Don't," she said, stopping him before he could touch her. "I can't—"

Booker dropped his ass to the carpet. "I won't..." he swallowed hard. "I won't touch you, but I need to know if you're hurt. Did he—"

"I'm fine. Bruised, but fine."

He pursed his lips and nodded, reminding himself that the guy who had hurt her was already dead. "All right, then. That's good."

"We need to get you to the hospital," she said softly. "You're bleeding."

He didn't realize she'd noticed. "I'm okay. It's better if we don't leave just yet. James should be here any minute and then we'll go."

She nodded and turned to rest a cheek on her knee.

How was he supposed to fix this? He couldn't change who he was. The things he'd done. "I'm sorry, Ellie. I wish you hadn't witnessed what I just did. I never want you to be afraid of—"

She looked at him then. "I stabbed him with a screwdriver," she blurted. Fresh tears sprang and ran down her cheeks.

Booker jerked back, surprised. For the first time, he noticed the blood on her fingers. "You did *what*?"

He glanced at Owen and saw the evidence for himself. A blue screwdriver handle dangling from Owen's side.

"I didn't have a choice," she whispered on a sob.

Relief washed through him as she scrambled for his lap. She wasn't afraid of him. She was afraid of herself.

Booker knew all too well what she was going through. Ellie hadn't killed Owen, but the intent had been there. Coming face-to-face with the realization that she had the capacity to take a life would be a real mind fuck.

He gathered her against his good side and held her while she cried. He kissed the top of her head. "You did the right thing and I'm proud of you. He didn't give you a choice. It was either him or you. And when those are the stakes, the answer is always you. Do you hear me? Always. You."

Two months later
Austin, Texas

BOOKER LEANED against the bumper of his truck, watching as Roman and Brandon loaded the last of the boxes into the moving van. His shoulder wound had healed, but he wasn't back to functioning at full capacity, making him extra grateful his buddies had shown up to help.

A door opened and Ellie stepped out of the house and into the garage. Booker took a moment to enjoy the sight of his wife while she was unaware.

His *wife*. Officially. Again. They had done the informal courthouse nuptials thing the previous week, neither of them wanting anything more than to be wed. They planned it specifically to coincide with his family's move to Montana. Two birds. One stone.

He was the luckiest man alive.

His family had welcomed Ellie back into the fold as though she'd never left. In a way, she hadn't. She had always been the one who held his heart. She made him whole. She made him happy. And he'd move hell and earth to make sure she was happy, too.

Ellie caught him staring and sauntered over.

"Hey, you." She walked into his waiting arms. "Noah rigged a laptop and has a ball game on. Ketcher said the steaks would be done in about ten minutes. Are you guys about done out here?"

He kissed her softly. "You're perfect, you know that?"

She laughed. "Because I offered you a ballgame and a steak?"

"Don't underestimate the power of good meat," Roman joked as he and Brandon joined them.

"Here, here," Brandon said.

Booker bent and put his mouth next to her ear. "No, *querida*," he said for her alone. "Because you're *breathing*."

He was just about to nuzzle her neck when he was rudely interrupted.

"All right, you two. That's enough," Brandon said, wiping the sweat from his face with a towel. "I have something to tell you."

Ellie stayed within the circle of his arms, but turned so she could face the other men. The position put her ass against his groin, so he wasn't about to complain.

"What'cha got?"

"The firm Ellie used to work for has hired Alec to do some forensic accounting of Owen's clients," Brandon said. "It appears Owen used some of the money that cycled through Dean Sanchez's businesses to fund his own political campaign."

Roman whistled. "Embezzling laundered money from a crime lord? That takes some balls."

Ellie tensed. "Dean is still in jail, though, right?"

"The combined evidence of what Alec uncovered with what the feds already had compelled the judge to deny bail, so yes. He's behind bars while he awaits trial, where odds are they will put him away for a long time."

Booker felt Ellie's muscles ease. Her chest deflated. "Then it was worth it."

They all knew what *it* was.

The first month after the *it*, Ellie had struggled. She had nightmares and bouts of self-doubt. Things were a little better now, and they'd keep getting better because his wife was a fucking rock star who could handle anything.

He bent and placed a kiss on the side of her neck. "I love you."

"I love you, too," she whispered back.

"Or for fuck's sake," Roman complained. "You two are the mushiest people I know."

Ellie escaped his arms and went to pat Roman on the cheek. "Your turn's coming."

"Forget it."

She glanced around. "Where are Adam and Sully?"

"Beer run," Booker told her. "They'll be back any minute."

"All right," Ellie said, walking backward toward the garage door. "You guys get your butts in the house when they get back, or your food will get cold. And I made a *tarta de queso* for dessert. *Abuelita*'s recipe. You won't want to miss it."

"What kind of tart?" Roman asked.

Booker shoved Roman's shoulder. "A Spanish cheese-cake, dumbass."

"Oh, God," Brandon groaned. "My favorite. With all of you moving away, it'll probably be the last time I'll get to have some. Unless ... are you sure I can't convince you to stay in Texas, Ellie?"

Ellie snagged Booker's gaze. She gave him a saucy wink.

"Sorry, Bran. Montana already made me an offer too tempting to refuse."

NOTE FROM PARKER

Thank you for reading *Tempting Montana*. I hope you enjoyed Booker and Ellie. If you could take a moment to leave a review, I'd be ever so grateful!

Do you like edge-of-your-seat-sexy romantic suspense, hot and steamy sports romance, and/or western romance? Be sure to check out my other books. There's no ... um ... shortage of dirty talking alpha men or feisty women who bring them to their knees! For a full list, visit my website: www.parkerkincade.com/books

There is more to come from The Martin Family and The Deadly Seven. Stay tuned! Be sure to subscribe to my newsletter for the latest news!

http://www.parkerkincade.com/Newsletter

Happy reading!
~Parker

She was there to work. He was there to play. Who says you can't mix business with pleasure?

Tropical paradise, bourbon, off-the-charts-sexual-chemistry ... what could possibly go wrong?

Please turn the page for a preview of Parker Kincade's fun-in-the-sun contemporary romance

Hot SEAL, Bourbon Neat

1

Paradise.

Asher "Knots" Dillon snorted to himself and raised the highball glass to his lips. The yellowish liquid barely resembled bourbon, but, hey, what did he expect from the land of rum and froufrou drinks?

The weather on Grand Turks was a balmy eighty-five degrees, the sun so bright he squinted behind his Oakleys. He took a healthy gulp, swirling the alcohol around his tongue until his tastebuds burned in protest. It really was horrible bourbon.

Christ. How the hell had he ended up here?

"Ash! Come on!"

Oh, right. Because his mom and sixteen-year old sister had planned this little vacay, and if being a Navy SEAL had taught him anything, it was that there was no fucking way the two most important women in his life were leaving the United States without protection. His mom, smart woman that she was, predicted his reaction and had booked a suite for him as well.

So, here he was. On leave at the Midnight Bay Beach

Resort in Turks and Caicos, where vacationers let loose, drank fruity drinks with ridiculous little adornments, and frolicked in the waves. *Frolicked*, for fuck's sake. Didn't people understand how dangerous the ocean could be? Oh, sure, it looked innocent enough, but Asher knew better than anyone that looks could be deceiving. Rip currents, shore-breaks, sharks—there were a thousand things that could go wrong when a person entered the water.

Asher cringed as he took another sip of the rotgut. He wasn't being fair. The general population wasn't being dumped into the middle of the ocean in the dead of night with a hundred pounds of gear strapped to their bodies. He got that. In his defense, any man who made it through Hell Week of BUD/S training lost some, if not all, love for the water. Any SEAL who said differently was a motherfucking liar. The ocean wasn't designed for recreation. It was deep and treacherous, with a mood that could change from calm to hell-on-earth in the space of a heartbeat.

And don't even get him started on the beach. His team had done enough time in the Gobi Desert that Asher swore he was still sweating sand out of his skin, months later.

His idea of a good time, this was not. Give him mountains and snow and a decent goddamn glass of bourbon...

Asher sighed.

Maybe next year.

"Asher!" Gracie bellowed again, drawing out his name as only a teenager could.

As he raised a hand to wave an *I see you. Carry on, preferably without me* to Gracie, he caught movement out of the corner of his eye. He glanced over in time to see a woman at a table not far from him surge to her feet. From his position behind her, Asher couldn't help but appreciate the view. Her light-colored hair was pulled into a ponytail. It ruffled in the breeze, teasing the golden skin between her shoulder blades. Her bathing suit was a one-piece that left her back exposed to the lower curve. And oh, what a back it was. Sleek and soft looking, with muscles that moved with elegant efficiency. She wore one of those oversized scarf-wrap things around her hips, but he could see enough of her legs to know she didn't need heels to give her the illusion of delicious length. She had it in spades.

Asher spent the day tossing out warning vibes to anyone who approached like they were beads at Mardi Gras, but if this woman had interrupted his solitude, he might've been inclined to ask her to join him. In his room. Naked.

"I'm good, thanks," the woman said, making Asher wonder what question he'd missed. Her voice had a vaguely familiar quality. Smooth as silk, with a steely-edged finish that caused a trail of pleasure to skirt down his spine.

He gave himself permission to revel in the sensation. Work kept him so busy lately that he'd neglected meeting any need that wasn't required to keep him alive. Now that he was on leave, he might have to see to his other, more carnal, needs.

"I've got a private cabana down the beach." The words dripped with innuendo, drawing Asher's attention away from the pretty lady to the guy standing in front of her. A surfer-blond college type. No more than twenty, twenty-one, tops. Fucking frat boy if Asher had ever seen one.

He looked like the other male vacationers on the beach with his bare chest and brightly colored board shorts. His head of messy curls needed a good shearing, and his expression was more leer than smile. The determined look in the frat boy's eyes said he wouldn't take no lightly. The way his friends were offering encouragement from a table close by proved the point.

Damn it. Was it too much to ask to enjoy his shitty bourbon in peace?

To her credit, the woman didn't back down. "No, thank you. As I said before, I'm fine right here."

"Oh, you're definitely fine." Frat boy's friends cheered and he tossed them a thumbs up.

Really, douche? No means no. Back away.

"I'm also definitely busy. I have work to do." She tried to step around him, but frat boy followed, squaring off with her. "If I could just..."

Frat boy spread his skinny arms. "Who works at the beach?"

"I do."

"Take a break then. Come on, sweet cheeks. Let's have some fun." Frat boy tipped a colorful girly drink to his lips. Not all of the slush made it into his mouth, though. He wiped away the portion sliding down his chin and then smeared it against his stomach with a smarmy grin.

"Want a taste of my drink? It's delicious."

Cue more laughter from the table o' asshole. A few of them high-fived.

Classy. Their parents should be so proud.

Asher couldn't take much more of this shit. Someone needed to teach these assholes some respect.

He glanced away long enough to check on his mom. She was right where Asher had left her, stretched out on a lounge chair with her nose in a book. He scanned the water for Gracie. It took him less than a minute to catch sight of her. Gracie bobbed and danced in the waves with a group of girls, her expression alight with youth and happiness. If Asher had his way, Gracie would never know anything but whatever she was feeling in that moment. He wasn't naive enough to believe he could shield her from the harshness of the world, but that didn't mean he wouldn't try.

Satisfied his mom was safe and Gracie wasn't falling prey to fucktard frat boys, Asher refocused on the activity within the beachside bar.

The kid hadn't given up.

"One drink," he begged.

"I'm sorry. Thank you for the offer, but I-I'm meeting someone."

Asher chuckled against the rim of his glass, liking her gumption. But if she wanted to be convincing about meeting someone, she shouldn't have made it sound as if she'd just had the greatest idea in the history of ideas. The little minx wasn't meeting anyone. She had just told one of those little white lies women used to get out of uncomfortable situations. Not that Asher blamed her. Frat boy was an ass.

The woman moved to step around frat boy again, and again the kid blocked her way.

"Excuse me. I need to order drinks for us. Not for you and me, us," she clarified. "Me and him, us. So, please. Let me by."

Frat boy reached out. The woman tried to bat his hand away, but frat boy dodged her attempt and latched on. Asher zeroed in on the fingers that curled into her golden skin and his blood pressure went on the rise. Persistence, however futile, was one thing. Touching was quite another.

Frat boy swayed his hips with the worst dirty dance move Asher had ever had the misfortune to witness.

"I've got drinks in my cabana." Frat boy licked his lips, his glance dropping to, Asher assumed, ogle the woman's tits. "Your friend can come. I don't mind sharing."

Frat boy clamped his other hand around her wrist and tugged her in close. Her audible gasp sealed the kid's fate.

"In fact..." Frat boy waved a come hither to some of his buddies. "I'll bring some friends, too. We'll make it a party."

Oh, you want to party, motherfucker?

Asher downed the rest of the bourbon and slid from the barstool.

Welcome to fucking paradise.

"LOOK..." The woman's voice was a mixture of exasperation and annoyance.

"Brett."

"Look, *Brett*. I appreciate the offer, but I really must decline." The last words were annoyingly polite, but pushed through clenched teeth. "I don't have time for this. I have work to do and my, um ... my boyfriend will be here any minute."

"Boyfriend?"

Frat boy really was daft. And he never saw Asher coming.

With a strike worthy of a cobra, Asher's hand engulfed Brett's forearm. He squeezed in just the right spot and...

"Ow! What the hell man!"

Brett's fingers shot open, releasing the woman with a reflexive jerk.

"I do believe the lady said no. If you're unfamiliar with the word, I'd be happy to give you a crash course."

"Who the fuck are you?"

Seemed frat boy hadn't bought her boyfriend story either. Asher released the kid with a little shove. "I'm the guy who's going to beat your sorry ass to a pulp if you don't step off."

Asher caught movement from the asshole table and

raised a palm toward Brett's buddies. "Stay where you are," he commanded, the transition from beach bum to SEAL as easy as breathing. "You don't want any of this."

Surprisingly enough, they heeded his warning. Seemed Brett's friends weren't as dumb as their buddy.

With the immediate threat averted, Asher finally turned his attention to the woman standing next to him. Eyes the color of frosted sapphires met his. His lungs heaved as recognition hit like a two-by-four to the gut.

Holy shit.

He would know those eyes anywhere. They'd been haunting his dreams, his fantasies, for years. It was *her*. Brooke Ramsey. His partner in a one-night stand that lasted for a glorious, sex-filled month. God, what had it been? Eight years?

Brooke's recollection was a split second behind his. Gratitude melted in a fiery blaze. If those icy blues could've shot laser beams, Asher would be dead where he stood. And maybe he was, because he never thought he'd see her again on this side of the pearly gates. That had been the plan anyway.

He almost couldn't believe it.

Asher shifted closer, hungry to take her in. She was still a beauty. Her hair wasn't just blonde. The wavy mass contained a plethora of yellow, gold, and red strands that glittered in the sun. Her striking eyes had golden lashes that wouldn't quit. She had delicate girl-next-door features, highlighted by an array of adorable freckles that dotted her nose and cheeks.

God, he'd missed those freckles.

Asher opened his mouth to ask if she was okay and instead heard himself say, "Hey, sweetheart. Sorry I'm late."

Brooke's smile was tight as she took a step back, then another, putting distance between them.

"Your timing couldn't be better, *babe*." Oh yeah. Little Miss Too Polite was pissed. And she had every right, truth be told. "I was on my way to the bar to get us a couple of drinks, but as you can see, I got held up."

"I can see that." Christ, she was cute. Asher didn't miss her quick intake of breath when he took her hand, and yeah, he felt it, too—the unmistakable zing of attraction he'd felt earlier, stronger now that they were touching. He brushed his thumb over her knuckles as he raised them to his lips. Damn, she smelled good. Tropical and completely edible.

She pulled her hand away with a nervous laugh. "So, ah, yeah." She hooked a thumb toward the bar. "I'll just go grab those drinks."

Asher hoped she didn't bring him one of those fruity frozen jobs, but it would look suspicious if he told her what to order. He'd just pretended to be her boyfriend. Drink preference was the kind of thing couples knew about each other, right? He didn't know. He didn't do the couple thing. Being a SEAL wasn't conducive to a lasting relationship. His own family was proof of that.

His dad had been a SEAL, gone more days than he was home, before being killed in action when Asher was sixteen. Gracie had still been in the womb, and his mom had nearly been destroyed. If she hadn't been close to giving birth, she might've let the grief take her. Even still, she'd walked around like a zombie for the first year. Asher helped where he could, but his mom struggled to raise an infant and a teenage boy on her own. She cried a lot back then, when she thought he couldn't hear.

Asher had joined the Navy when it became obvious he

wasn't cut out for college. He worked his ass off and became a SEAL at age twenty-four. His primary objective was to ensure his mom and sister were taken care of, but where he'd followed his dad's footsteps into the Navy, he wouldn't follow them into marriage. No way he would put a woman through what his dad put his mom through. The constant disappearances. The cancelled plans. The lengthy deployments. The stress over the dangerous job, a job Asher happened to love. It was easier to remain unattached.

What he did couldn't be considered dating. If he met a woman he found attractive and if she wanted to play, he was up front about expectations before the clothes came off. Lots of orgasms. Nothing more. Well, maybe dinner, before or after the sex. He wasn't a complete jackass.

"Would you like anything special this time?" Brooke asked and Asher had the urge to kiss her. He resisted, since he was pretty sure she'd punch him.

He shook his head and glanced pointedly at the glass in Brett's hand. "You know I don't go for that girly shit. Bourbon, neat, is always gonna be my drink of choice, sweetheart." He tried to sound apologetic, as if this was a discussion they'd had before.

"Right. A real man's man, aren't you, *babe*." Then, she surprised the hell out of him by rising up on her toes and whispering a breathy "Thank you," close to his ear. Her lips caressed his cheek for the briefest of moments before she moved away.

The nearness of her mouth to any part of his body lit him up like the night sky on the Fourth of July. Made him want to get reacquainted in a down and dirty kind of way.

"Hurry back." Asher tipped his head, watching as she weaved through the tables. Once she was safely placing their orders with the bartender, he turned back to Brett, whose stupid ass was still hanging around.

Asher straightened, dwarfing the kid. He crossed his arms, knowing the pose would make his biceps bulge in all the right places. He wasn't above posturing if a guy had the size or bulk to back it up. He happened to have both.

"You wanna explain what you were doing with your hands all over my girl?"

Brett squared his shoulders. "Don't have a cow, man. We were just looking to have a little fun."

Have a cow? The kid deserved to get his ass kicked for that expression alone.

"Did she look like she was having fun to you?" Asher knew what kind of *fun* frat boy and his douchebags were looking for, and it boiled his blood.

Frat boy smirked. "We would've made it good for her."

Asher dropped the pussy with one punch.

"Unless you wanna wear your blood on the outside, I wouldn't try it," Asher cautioned the four guys at the asshole table who rose to their feet. The group varied in size, but Asher had no doubt he could take them if they were stupid enough to come at him. Keeping an eye on the group, he held a palm out to stay the now-concerned bartender and a wide-eyed Brooke. He had this. He didn't need their interference.

On the ground, Brett groaned as his friends argued in hushed tones.

They were starting to attract a crowd. A few passers-by stopped in the sand. A couple of the beachgoers craned their necks around lounge chairs to see what was going on. Asher needed to shut this shit down before his mom and sister came running. He didn't want either one of them anywhere near these bozos.

"What's the play here, boys?" Asher asked, giving them a chance to step up or step out.

"We don't want any trouble," one of them finally said, stepping forward to help Brett to his feet.

Asher addressed the whole group. "Let me be very clear. Touch my girl again..." he thought about Gracie and amended, "Touch *any* girl at this resort without permission, and you'll limp back to your mommy's and daddy's. You get me?" He eyeballed Brett. "That cabana down the beach you were bragging about? You should go there. Now."

A few curse words were mumbled as the boys hit the sand. Since there was no fucking wall to place his back against, Asher took the chair at Brooke's table that allowed him the best view of the retreating group. They were headed down the beach in the opposite direction of the hotel when Brooke returned to the table. She clunked his bourbon down hard enough to crack the mosaic table top. Seemed the glass was as stout as the rotgut, since both held steady.

Brooke slipped into the chair across from him. Her drink got a more delicate treatment. She sipped from the tall glass that had a sprig of mint on the top and then set it on a napkin. She rested her forearms against the table and laced her fingers around the glass, seemingly not inclined to talk around an elephant the size of Texas.

Tension charged the air between them, making his skin prickle with awareness and his hands eager to get reacquainted with her body. It seemed when it came to Brooke Ramsey, nothing had changed. Asher had been with his share of women, but Brooke was the only one who ever triggered his inner caveman. Triggered ideas like *mine* and *forever*. The only woman who ever tempted him to throw aside his beliefs about relationships and give one a try. So he left.

The only thing harder than walking away would've been to stay with the knowledge that one day this beautiful creature would suffer heartache, and it would be all his fault.

Asher cleared his throat. Brooke's gaze met his over the rim of the highball. What did one say to the woman he spent a month fucking nine ways to Sunday before bugging out of her life in the dead of night?

And then it hit him.

"In all the gin joints..." he started, remembering her love for the movie *Casablanca*. It was her favorite. She also loved custard-filled pastries, preferred tea over coffee, and had a kinky side that included being restrained in bed.

He grinned at that last bit. Asher earned his nickname with legitimate, work-related tasks, but his ability to tie a decent knot had started with her. Everything started with her.

He'd done the right thing, hadn't he? He'd been so sure at the time. Seeing her now, though, all golden-skinned and beautiful...

"In all the towns..." he continued, knowing the line by heart.

Brooke's laugh was the greatest sound he'd ever heard. A little light, a little grumbly, and a whole lot of sexy. It was the kind of laugh that lit up her face. The kind that made everyone within earshot smile along with her.

He could listen to that sound for the rest of his life.

Fuck.

ABOUT THE AUTHOR

USA Today Bestselling author Parker Kincade is known for her award-winning, edge-of-your-seat-sexy romantic suspense, hot and steamy sports romance, and contemporary western romance. She lives in the southern United States where she spends her days spoiling her beloved boxer, enjoying life as a grandparent, and dreaming up sexy alpha men for the next adventure. Learn more about Parker Kincade at www.parkerkincade.com.

To receive an email when Parker releases a new book, sign up for her newsletter!

http://www.parkerkincade.com/newsletter

ALSO BY PARKER KINCADE

The Martin Family

One Night Stand

Shadow of Sin

No Control (Deadly Seven Crossover)

Tempting Montana (Deadly Seven Crossover)

Ties That Burn (TBD)

Midnight Tidings (TBD)

The Deadly Seven

No Control (Martin Family Crossover)

Tempting Montana (Martin Family Crossover)

Saving Kate (TBD)

SEALs in Paradise

Hot SEAL, Bourbon Neat

Game On

Spring Training

Southern Heat

Wild Catch (formerly Dare's Wild: TBD)

Devon's Fall (TBD)

Shadow Maverick Ranch

White Collar Cowboy

Borrowed Cowboy

Cowboy Redeemed

White Collar Wedding (short story)

Shadow Maverick Ranch Boxed Set (Book 1-3)

Short Stories

Devlin

Two of Cups (Love in the Cards Anthology)